KILL FOF ~~~AN!

G000245952

GRINDHOUSE PRESS

BRYAN SMITH

Grindhouse Press
PO BOX 521
Dayton, Ohio 45401

Grindhouse Press #042
ISBN-10: 1-941918-35-2
ISBN-13: 978-1-941918-35-7

DEDICATION

In memory of Molly

Other titles by Bryan Smith

ONE

Followers of the dark faith began to gather at the designated meeting spot deep in the woods in the hour before midnight. It was the night before Halloween and there was a certain uncanny magic in the air, a sense of something momentous about to occur. Something special and life-altering. Each of the gathered acolytes felt it deep in their bones. There had been no promise of anything of the sort at the most recent gathering, thus none of them had any reason to expect anything beyond the usual prior to entering the woods that night.

Not that they would have needed such a promise to entice them into attending the monthly midnight mass, which was always plenty exciting even without the prospect of something extra. Each mass centered around a blood sacrifice ceremony, which was followed by a wanton orgy around a blazing bonfire. Ritual murder and a subsequent descent into uninhibited hedonism would normally be an impossible act to follow.

Yet that sense of being on the cusp of something of great import was undeniable. A quiet sense of solemn duty was the normal way of things in the moments before the beginning of each mass. The faithful usually did not interact with each other as they made their way to the big clearing where the monthly ceremonies were always held. It was a time for silent introspection.

Tonight was different. It felt that way to each of the acolytes from the moment they entered the woods. The air felt charged. Alive with something strange and exciting. Something from beyond the natural world. The kinship that always existed between them felt stronger than ever, magnified a thousand-fold. They were collectively in on something that would change their lives forever. What that might be was yet unknown, but the mystery at the heart of what they were all feeling heightened the overriding sense of elation. The autumn evening was crisply cold, but the chill was barely felt as the faithful continued the newly joyful march through the woods, a pleasant warmth suffusing them long before they reached the clearing and the bonfire already burning there.

Micah Russo was one of the newest members of the unholy congregation. Tonight's mass would only be his second. He'd been enticed into joining the faith by the girl he was dating, a pale-skinned and dark-haired gothic beauty he'd met at the new record store in town a couple months back. Her delicately pretty features and quirky personal style had entranced him from the start. She dressed all in black all the time. Her fingers and the backs of her hands were heavily tattooed with occult symbols. Another tattoo, this one a portrait-quality rendering of Vampira, adorned her upper right arm. The jewelry she wore included skull rings and severed head earrings. Cynthia Winthrop was her given name, but she preferred the alternate moniker Sindie Midnight. It was the name she used for promoting her art. Micah's mother never called his girlfriend by either name, instead referring to her most often as "that spooky little bitch".

She was always after him to dump Sindie and date a more normal girl, but for Micah that wasn't even close to being an option. He was too much under her spell, hopelessly enthralled by everything about her. There was nothing he wouldn't do for her, no sacrifice he wouldn't make on her behalf. His intensity of feeling was matched—and perhaps even exceeded—by what she felt for him. She told him they would someday marry little more than a week after they met, after which she gave him money to buy her an engagement ring.

Micah was embarrassed because he was unemployed and barely had any money of his own. He felt he should get a job and buy her a ring after he'd legitimately earned some cash. She told him she didn't want that. Between her job at the record store and her rapidly increasing income from selling her macabre artwork, she made more than enough money for both of them. A job would only distract him from devoting every waking minute of every day to worshipping her.

"I'm all you need," she told him. "All you'll *ever* need."

That was all he needed to hear. He dropped all pretense of taking on anything resembling a traditional male role in the relationship, deferring to Sindie in all matters and never voicing disagreement with her about anything. He did all this without regret and had no sense of anything being even slightly amiss until the night she told him about her devotion to Satan.

At first he didn't quite understand what she was telling him. He thought she maybe belonged to one of these modern so-called "Satanic" groups that didn't actually believe in the existence of any demonic evil entity. He was aware of those groups from things on the internet. They used Satan as a provocative and subversive means of delivering progressive messages. They were social activists, not true devotees of the dark path.

As it turned out, Sindie was not talking about groups like that.

Quite the contrary.

She believed wholeheartedly in the existence of Satan, and that he actively worked to spread evil throughout the world with the aim of eventually bringing about the fall of mankind. Even after she told him this, he wasn't sure he believed her. She was playing with him. Telling an elaborate joke. She insisted otherwise, but he continued clinging to this idea until she took him to his first midnight mass a month ago. On that night, he was thoroughly and permanently disabused of the notion. When it came to the dark lord, she was absolutely a true believer, as were all the other members of the unholy congregation.

In the early stages of that first mass, he persisted in believing it was an essentially harmless activity. He thought of it as Satanic cosplay. That illusion ended with the blood sacrifice. A beautiful but drugged-looking young woman was dragged into the clearing and placed on the altar. Another woman approached the altar and stood over the drugged woman. This other woman wore a long velvet cape and nothing beneath. A white plague mask with a long beak covered the top half of her face. The sight of her large breasts and shapely body stirred something shameful in Micah. Shameful because it was the first flicker of lust he'd felt for anyone other than Sindie since they'd started dating. It was confusing because it felt like an intrusion on the all-consuming connection they shared.

"Who is that?" he asked her.

Sindie smiled but didn't look at him. Her gaze was riveted to the ceremony. "The priestess," came her whispered reply.

Then she shushed him with a finger pressed to her lips.

The priestess had a strange-looking dagger. It had an ornate hilt and a long blade forged to mimic the form of a slithering snake. As Micah watched with dawning trepidation, she raised the dagger high over her head. A chant rose up from the congregation. *Hail Satan, glorious and strong. Hail Satan, master of all.* It went on like that with multiple variations. Some Latin phrases were mixed in. The chanting was pretty evil-sounding out there in the dark woods, but Micah also thought it a bit silly, like something out of a cheesy made-for-TV movie from the '70s about Satanic school girls.

That impression lasted until the priestess brought the dagger viciously downward. The blade pierced the drugged girl's abdomen. Blood gushed out of the wound when the priestess yanked it out again. The girl on the altar came out of her stupor as the pain ripped through her. She screamed and tried to sit up, but the priestess brought the dagger down again, this time plunging it in just beneath the woman's sternum. The priestess stabbed the woman several more times, continuing even after she'd stopped moving. By the time she was finished, the front of her body was coated in gore. She stepped back and two male members of the congregation came forward. A box was set on the altar. Inside it were the tools of a coroner. The dead woman's chest was opened and her ribs cracked and spread apart. Her heart was then surgically removed and presented to the priestess, who held it over her head and said some stuff about honoring Satan while begging him to accept this sacrifice as proof of the congregation's devotion.

Micah was stunned.

No part of him had expected to see an actual murder that night. Realizing he was among a large group of dangerous people unlikely to be sympathetic, he worked hard to keep his shock contained. When Sindie gave him a look of expectant delight, he somehow summoned a fake smile. He tried hard to make her think he was as into what was happening as she was. Deception on a scale so big wasn't normally something he could manage, but he was aided by the even bigger distraction that followed.

Members of the congregation were required to disrobe upon

entering the so-called "sacred circle", their name for the clearing where their gatherings were held. They then donned robes and gathered around the large wooden platform upon which the altar rested. All acolytes had brought along their own ankle-length hooded robes, it seemed. Sindie had one for him and a smaller one for herself. Wearing his robe that night, Micah felt like a fraud. He wasn't anything close to being a real Satanist, not even the pretend kind. Unfortunately, it seemed he was in love with one.

After the priestess droned on a while longer about how awesome Satan was, the people around him began to remove their robes. Soon every one of them, even Sindie, was standing naked in the clearing. He was the only one still wearing his robe, which was damn awkward. Everyone else was staring at him. Wilting beneath the attention, he reluctantly removed his robe and stood naked under the moonlight with the rest of them.

Sindie had been watching him in a way that could be interpreted as at least mildly distrusting, but when the robe came off, she smiled and nodded in approval. Then she went over to another attractive young woman and started making out with her. She reached between the girl's legs and slid her fingers into her pussy. Soon they were rolling around on the ground together. This produced yet another moment of profound and dizzying shock for Micah. His girlfriend, the person he loved more than anyone else in the world, was suddenly fucking some chick he'd never seen before right in front of him. He felt hurt and betrayed. He had tears in his eyes. The hurt was tempered somewhat when he realized similar things were happening all around him. Everywhere he looked, people were copulating. Every possible sexual combination was on open, brazen display.

He remembered thinking, *Holy shit, it's a fucking orgy!*

An older lady he recognized as one of his teachers from high school came over and grabbed him by the dick. The woman was maybe thirty years his senior and had large, saggy tits, but he was stunned to realize he was rock hard. She turned around and pushed her ass at him, inviting him to penetrate her from behind. He did so at once, twisting his head around to watch what Sindie was doing to that girl while he banged the shit out of his old algebra teacher. The teacher's pussy was not the last his cock penetrated that night. There were several others, including that of Sindie's first partner of the night. At one point he saw Sindie getting double-teamed by a pair of muscular guys and felt another flare of jealousy and anger.

Then, from seemingly out of nowhere, the priestess was standing before him. No longer wearing the cape, but with the top part of her face still obscured by the creepy white plague mask. Her torso was swathed in gore. She grabbed him by the throat and rode him to the ground, mounting him and riding his dick in a ferocious frenzy while maintaining her hold on his throat. The sway and jiggle of her tits was hypnotic. While he was inside the priestess, his dick felt huge, like some kind of monstrous super dick. Which was weird, because he was pretty sure his penis size was roughly average. The ecstasy was so intense it made him cry. Their coupling seemed to go on forever while the orgy swirled around them. There was no room in his head for anything other than the priestess and what she was doing to him. When she finally slapped him and told him to come, he screamed and felt like his whole body was exploding. The sensation was consciousness-obliterating. The world went away for a bit. When it came back into focus, the priestess was gone. He looked for her and couldn't find her. He wandered around the sacred circle looking for her, feeling forlorn and lost.

Eventually, Sindie caught up to him and thrust his regular clothes into his hands. Only then did he realize the orgy was over. People were getting dressed and slipping away into the woods. Micah was confused. It was as if a spell had been broken. He thought about all the people he'd copulated with that night and couldn't believe it. How he'd managed to keep going all that time without coming until the priestess commanded it was baffling. It didn't seem possible and yet he knew it had happened. He asked Sindie about it, but she told him she didn't want to talk about it until they were out of the woods.

Even later, though, she never provided any real answers, except to say it was all about glorifying Satan and expressing contempt for God's laws. That part he could grasp on a theoretical level, even if it was batshit crazy, but he still couldn't wrap his head around so many other things. How he'd wound up fucking so many people he would normally have no desire to fuck, for example. It was as if his own will had been suspended and overridden by some outside imperative. By some outside *consciousness.* It freaked him out.

He told himself he'd never let Sindie drag him to another midnight mass in the fucking woods, even if she threatened to break up with him over it. He was still crazy about her, but that sense of losing control of his own body and mind was something he never wanted to experience again. Nor did he have any desire to ever again be among a group of people who stood by and watched while an innocent woman got murdered, then seemed to *revel* in it.

He tried to put the whole thing out of his mind, but was only partially successful. During the daytime, when he was hanging out at the record store with Sindie, he was mostly able to avoid thinking about it. He listened to music and looked at records while talking to Sindie about mundane things. What they might name their kids someday, if they ever had any. The house they would get once she became rich and famous for her art. These were all pleasant distractions that allowed him the illusion of things being normal.

At night it was different. The priestess haunted his dreams. She did things to him. Unspeakably vile and degenerate things that nonetheless felt so good. On several occasions he'd wake up to find the bedsheets stained with his nocturnal emissions. If she noticed this, Sindie never said anything about it.

Then it started to get toward late October. The time for the next mass was approaching. Sindie reminded him it was coming up and they would definitely be attending. Micah attempted to tell her of his resolve to never go again, but she told him to shut up with that nonsense. He was going, end of story. The lethal look in her eyes as she said this was enough to convince him to withhold any further gestures of defiance.

He was feeling desperate by the time the day of the mass came around. The hours kept slipping away and before he knew it he was walking through the woods with Sindie. He felt small and powerless. It was all going to happen again and there was no way he could stop it. A small spark of defiance ignited in his brain. There was still time to turn around and run out of these woods. He had a will of his own, feeble though it seemed at times. All he had to do was exercise it and leave all this insanity behind forever. He could take Sindie's Kia Sorrento and some of her money and flee town. Or he could move back in with his mother and start going to church every Sunday, maybe devote himself to Jesus and spend his days begging for forgiveness for his sins.

Then he felt it.

That strange charge in the air. The pleasant way it seemed to suffuse every pore of his body. Before long he became aware of the dopey grin on his face. He looked at Sindie and said, "Do you feel that? What the hell is that?"

She smiled and squeezed his hand. "The presence of Satan. I've only felt it once before, but it's something you never forget. There's nothing like it. Nothing as good. Not even fucking close."

"The actual *devil* is here tonight?"

The hopeful note in his voice astonished Micah in the wake of his earlier thoughts, but it was definitely there.

Sindie squeezed his hand again. "Yes. I'm glad you're here with me for this."

"So am I. I love you."

Sindie tugged at his hand and turned him toward her, raising up on her toes to kiss him on the mouth. "I love you, too, baby. Hail Satan."

TWO

Micah's second midnight mass was similar to his first only in the sense that it featured a blood sacrifice at the beginning. Another drugged-out young woman was brought into the clearing and placed on the altar. The priestess came out of the woods and climbed the platform's steps to stand above the altar with the strange snake dagger in hand. Once again, she was wearing only the long velvet cape and white plague mask that covered the top half of her face. Micah's cock stiffened instantly at the sight of her. As before, the hooray-for-Satan chants started up as the woman raised the dagger high over her head.

This time, however, he experienced none of the disbelief and trepidation he'd felt the last time. There was no sense of horror at the plight of the sacrificial victim on the altar. A collective giddiness permeated the air. Micah looked around and saw people smiling beneath the cowls of their robes. Somewhere out in the midst of all that Satanic humanity, a girl couldn't stop giggling. Micah soon found himself giggling, too. Then he burst out laughing when the dagger arced downward and the tip of the blade plunged into one of the victim's breasts. He wasn't the only one. A lot of the faithful were laughing. The sound of hysterical laughter only grew louder as the woman on the altar squirmed and attempted—to no avail, of course—to get away from the knife.

On a disconnected level, he remained aware of how absurd, obscene, and horrific this vicious murder was, especially juxtaposed against all this uncontrolled hilarity. Knowing this, however, did nothing to dampen what he was feeling. He felt connected to the people around him in a way he hadn't last time. They were drawing energy from each other and recirculating that energy in a way that felt like a deep immersion into some kind of dark magic. Yes, magic. Micah could think of no other word that applied. He felt enveloped in it. A vibrating field of invisible power. It was more intoxicating than any drug on earth. Micah found himself wishing he could live inside this feeling forever.

Hail Satan!

The priestess continued to hack away at the busty blonde beauty on the altar. Had he really thought she attacked the victim in a frenzied manner last time? Because after this he was going to have to reassess his definition of frenzied. The lady was going wild with that fucking dagger. She was like a beast. Like a thing possessed. At one point she leaned over the altar and ripped away a piece of bloody tit meat with her teeth. Micah watched in awe and appreciation as she swallowed the piece of flesh whole. After that she continued to hack away at the now definitely dead victim with wild abandon for several more minutes. By the time she stopped, the dead thing on the altar scarcely resembled anything human. Even the face had been mangled beyond recognition.

Then she dropped the dagger and plunged both of her hands deep into the dead woman's shredded abdominal cavity and reached up under her ribcage. The strength on display as she rooted around inside the body and eventually ripped out the woman's heart was stupefying. No coroner tools were necessary this time. Micah couldn't imagine any woman possessing the necessary strength for a thing like that, not even the musclebound bodybuilder type of gal, and this woman looked nothing like that. For that matter, he had a hard time envisioning any man being able to do it. He was pretty sure tearing a human body apart wasn't nearly as easy as zombies made it look in the movies. It would require an unnatural level of strength.

The priestess removed her cape and climbed atop the altar to stand before the gathered acolytes with the blood-dripping heart clutched tightly in her raised right hand. She looked like an ancient barbarian woman holding aloft the severed head of a defeated enemy. This impression was banished about a second after it formed in Micah's head, because that was when he began to perceive the glow emanating from the eyes and open mouth of the priestess. This light intensified quickly and soon was brighter by far than the light cast by the flames of the bonfire. It pierced the evening sky like searchlights.

As Micah watched this with mounting awe tinged with an underlying, respectful fear, he realized an earlier thought of his was far more accurate than his barbarian queen impression. She was possessed. There was something inside her that wasn't human. That was the source of the unnatural level of strength. It was a demon. A ghost.

Or …

Satan.

All doubt was dispelled when the entity inside the priestess began to speak in a thunderous, stentorian voice. That sense of overpowering elation and ecstasy ramped relentlessly upward as the assembled acolytes listened to the darkly wondrous things their master had to say. He had come among them to deliver a message and send them on a mission. Each acolyte was charged with the task of bringing the devil as many pure souls as possible, from which he would draw immense power. The souls of those not yet touched by sin. Those who had not yet known the pleasures of the flesh. The more pure souls his followers delivered, the greater their eventual reward.

Tomorrow was Halloween.

And on that day the devil's faithful were to go out into their various communities and kill.

Kill all the virgins.

With the message delivered, the supernatural light faded from the eyes of the priestess. The consciousness of the woman behind the mask reassumed control of her body. The heart of tonight's victim was still clutched in her hand. She brought the organ to her mouth and slowly lapped the blood from it with her preternaturally long tongue in a way Micah found overpoweringly erotic.

Then she smiled and summoned the faithful to the altar, where they were to taste the blood and flesh of the innocent, pure soul taken that night. This, they were told, would give them the ability to identify other pure souls by sight. One by one, the acolytes climbed the steps to the platform to taste the dead woman's blood and devour bits of her flesh. By the time each member of the congregation had finished taking a taste, not much was left of the corpse.

Next the robes came off and the acolytes went at each other with their usual level of utter abandon. An attractive girl was standing nearby. She had cherry-red hair and luscious bee-stung lips. Sindie grabbed her and threw her to the ground. Then she pounced on her. Micah made no move toward any of the many potential partners in the vicinity. He fended off several advances while keeping his gaze on the priestess. She would come to him soon. He was certain of it.

She did not disappoint him.

THREE

The twice-weekly meetings of the Youth Abstinence League of Littleburg (commonly known by its acronym, YALL) were held each Wednesday and Sunday. Membership consisted almost entirely of teenagers from devoutly religious families. Some belonged to the group because they sincerely wanted to preserve their virginity until they were married, believing it was what Jesus wanted of them. Most of the kids in this category would sooner blind themselves by shoving fire-heated pokers slowly through their eyeballs than risk doing anything that might endanger their future in heaven.

Other members of the group did not possess these beliefs. They were there because it was what their devoutly religious parents wanted. A stranger walking into any given meeting of YALL would be able to instantly identify members in this second category. They were the obviously unhappy ones. Kids who desperately wished they could be anywhere else doing anything else. They lived under a cloak of oppression, going through the motions of pretending to believe things their parents told them they should believe while yearning for the day when they would be free to make their own decisions about faith and live life for themselves.

Seth Thornton had been forced to join the group three months ago, after his mother walked into his room unannounced and caught him masturbating to a lesbian porn video on his laptop. She screamed and went running out of the room to fetch her husband. An aggravated Seth hurriedly clicked out of the video and put his wilting junk away, managing to get zipped up before his father came charging into the room. The man's face was red with rage. Before Seth could say a word in his own defense, his dad's huge fist crashed across his jaw, knocking him to the floor.

The blow was hard enough to make him woozy and he needed a minute to clear his head. His father continued to scream at him while his mother stood outside his bedroom door and wailed like a grief-stricken widow at a funeral. The things his father was screaming at him were just noise in those first moments after being hit. A muffled roar coming from somewhere far away. Then the fog finally cleared enough for him to understand.

"*What do you have to say for yourself!?*" his father screamed. "*What do you have to say for yourself!?*"

Just those same words over and over, like a scratchy old record stuck on a groove.

A trickle of blood slid down Seth's chin as he managed to raise his head off the floor and stare blearily at his father. "I'll never forget to lock my door again. That's what I have to say for myself."

His father's face got even redder—a thing Seth wouldn't have thought possible—as he called his son an insolent little brat. At that point he began to remove his belt. The prolonged whipping that ensued was something Seth would never forget. That was the day he realized he would always hate his father. One day he would move far away and never again see either of his parents. He would try to forget they even existed.

For now, though, he had no choice but to live by their rules and accept the punishment they deemed necessary for his transgression. In discussing the incident with them afterward, he learned the act of masturbation alone wasn't the big issue for them. They didn't approve of it, but by itself it would have been a minor problem. He was a teenaged boy. Teenagers did such things. Sometimes they just couldn't help it, despite it being shameful in the eyes of God.

The thing that really upset them was what he had been watching while pleasuring himself. His mother sobbed as she recounted the horror she'd felt at seeing the images of two women having sex with each other. Seth's father glared at him and shook his head in disgust. They told him homosexuality in any form was a sin, even when it involved two women rather than two men. He was probably already doomed to hell just for having watched the video, but they said they loved him anyway and weren't ready to give up on him just yet.

Worried he was on the brink of heading down a slippery slope of sin and depravity, his parents insisted he attend religious counseling sessions every week. He was also ordered to join YALL. These were non-negotiable requirements for remaining in their house. If he failed to do what they wanted, he would be kicked out and left to fend for himself, something he wasn't quite capable of doing just yet. Seth wasn't completely sure they had any real legal basis to do that. He was still a minor, after all, and wouldn't reach legal adult status for almost another year. But this was a mid-sized town in the Bible Belt. Legal or not, he was at the mercy of his parents in this matter.

So here he was on yet another Wednesday afternoon after school, sitting in his car in the parking lot outside the church where YALL held its twice-weekly meetings in the basement. This was never a fun time for him, but this week the Wednesday meeting happened to fall on Halloween. He'd rather be at home watching the horror movie marathon on Channel 39. Other kids his age would be going to haunted houses or costume parties. He'd love nothing more than to hang out with his friends later tonight. They could walk around the neighborhood and soak in the spooky atmosphere. His parents, however, did not approve of Halloween celebrations of any type, which they deemed pagan and evil.

Of fucking course.

His car's engine was running and the radio was tuned to the static-riddled signal of a distant classic rock station, the only thing he considered remotely listenable on the AM/FM dial. The car was a decades-old Subaru with an ugly tan paint job speckled with rust. Even if he still had a phone, he wouldn't be able to pair it with the ancient radio via Bluetooth and stream better music. His parents had confiscated his phone and laptop after the masturbation incident. These things provided easy access to sources of corruption and he clearly could not be trusted with them.

It was all so endlessly and profoundly frustrating for Seth. He was chafing under the mental strain of all the extreme restrictions placed on his existence. His parents were oppressed idiots suffering from a deeply rooted form of religious mania they would take with them to their graves. Escape was all he wanted, but it was beyond reach for now. He couldn't just drive his car out of town and leave all this crap behind. The Subaru wasn't reliable and he doubted he'd get very far before it broke down. Besides that, he had no money and nowhere to go.

I'm fucking stuck.

He sighed resignedly.

Oh, well. Might as well get this over with.

He shut off the Subaru's engine and reached for the door handle. Before he could open the door, he glanced at his rearview mirror and caught a glimpse of another car pulling into the parking lot. His breath caught in his throat and his heart started beating faster. The car was one he recognized, a yellow Mini

Cooper with two vertical black stripes on the hood that made it look sort of like an enormous, motorized bumble bee. It belonged to Caitlin Winthrop, who'd gotten it as a sweet sixteen gift from her parents.

Seth's hand remained on the door handle as he watched Caitlin's Mini zoom past him and pull to a stop in a space near the entrance to the church. She got out a moment later, wearing a white button-down top and a short, pleated skirt. Seth felt a surge of lust as he watched her walk down the sidewalk toward the entrance. He grimaced and squirmed uncomfortably in his seat.

Caitlin was the sexiest girl Seth had ever seen, either on TV or in real life. Or on the internet, for that matter. There wasn't a porn babe alive who could compare to Caitlin. She was his dream girl. Too bad she barely knew he existed. She was a snooty rich bitch who never even looked at him during YALL meetings. Even more confounding was her apparent genuine devotion to premarital abstinence. How could she look that amazing and not be an unstoppable sexual dynamo?

It was a fucking mystery.

Sighing again, Seth got out of the car and followed Caitlin into the church.

FOUR

Earlier in the day ...

The alarm on his phone went off at noon. Micah groaned and rolled onto his side to reach for it, his hand fumbling around on the nightstand until he was able to grip the phone and hit the stop button. With the annoying tone of the alarm silenced, he groaned and sat up, swinging his legs over the side of the bed.

He looked around and realized Sindie wasn't in the room with him. Not a big deal or source of concern. She almost always woke up before he did, sometimes hours earlier. He would most likely find her in their apartment's spare bedroom, a space she used as her art studio. She typically worked on her art in the morning before going off to her afternoon shift at the record store. Thinking he would go peek in for a look at her current work-in-progress, he got up and pulled on some sweatpants.

After yawning and stretching, he walked out of the bedroom and down the hall. The door to the spare bedroom was standing open. He peeked in and frowned when he saw Sindie wasn't in there. An unfinished painting depicting naked Satanists frolicking around a bonfire sat on an easel in the middle of the room. Like all her work, it was visually striking and vividly rendered. As always, he was impressed. Lately she'd been selling every piece she completed. Sometimes an individual piece would fetch a sum that was more than their monthly rent. At this point, the record store income was just a bonus. Micah truly believed she would be famous someday.

Then he flashed back to last night's Satanic mass. His frown deepened as he remembered the murderous mission he and the other members of the congregation had been assigned at the end of the blood ceremony. He cringed at the memory of eating bits of the sacrificial victim's flesh, his stomach twisting as he recalled the physical sensation of the bloody meat sliding down his throat. He'd reveled in it at the time. It was as if he'd been drugged, as if he'd been a different person entirely. Now, though, he only felt sick.

Sweat broke out on his brow and a moment later Micah was running back down the hall to the bathroom. He got there in time to drop to his knees in front of the toilet, raise the lid, and vomit into the bowl. The puke came out in a hot rush, striking the water hard enough to make droplets of it splash against his face. He heaved a few more times before his stomach ceased convulsing. Wiping the sweat from his forehead, he stared at the mess in the toilet bowl and wondered if any of what he was seeing consisted of partially digested pieces of human flesh.

Probably.

This unpleasant truth made his stomach twist again.

"What's going on in here?"

Sindie was standing just inside the bathroom's open door. Wearing only a pair of tiny black cotton shorts and a sleeveless black t-shirt with the Cradle of Filth logo on the front, she struck a disapproving pose, glaring at him with her arms folded beneath her breasts.

"Did you hear me, Micah?"

He nodded and shakily wiped more sweat from his brow. "Yeah. Sorry. I'm just not feeling that great suddenly."

"Okay, but you need to get your shit together. We need to get out there and start collecting souls."

Micah grimaced. "Are we really still doing that?"

Sindie's glare intensified. "Of course we are. Now get up and get out here. There's something you need to see."

And with that she was gone, backing out of the bathroom and heading back down the hall to the living room. Her demeanor clearly indicated she had no interest in debating the subject with him. The leaving without a word thing was a tactic she'd used frequently during their months together, her way of completely shutting down any potential disagreement. Early on he'd learned the wisdom of never trying to press a point when she did this.

He had a sick feeling he'd have to make an exception to that rule today. If he couldn't talk Sindie out of embarking on a murder spree, the bright future of fame and fortune he believed was her destiny might never come to pass. You couldn't just go out and brazenly kill a bunch of people without being caught and thrown in jail. Jail wasn't even the worst possible outcome. They might get gunned down by the police. A would-be victim might kill them in an act of self-defense. There were so many ways it could all go horribly wrong. In fact, he couldn't imagine any way this whole thing could end well.

Micah flushed the toilet and got shakily to his feet. He went over to the wash basin and turned on the cold water tap. After splashing some water on his face, he plucked a hand towel from a hook on the wall, patted his skin dry, and went out to the living room feeling determined. He had to talk some sense into Sindie. He loved her and wanted that bright future for her more than anything, but an insidious brand of craziness was consuming her life and he was the only person with even a remote chance of turning her in a different direction.

She was standing at the big window in the living room, staring intently at something down in the parking lot. She looked enthralled. Captivated. Bursting with barely contained energy. They lived on the third floor of building G in the Crestview apartment complex. The view out this window wasn't a particularly exciting one. Mostly all you could see were other buildings in the sprawling complex, which was the largest of its kind in

Littleburg. From this vantage point, it looked as if it stretched out into eternity. Micah couldn't imagine what she was looking at that could be so fascinating.

Her head snapped in his direction as she sensed his presence. "Get the fuck over here, Micah. You *have* to see this."

He sighed and went over to the window, his sense of trepidation growing with each step closer. "Look, Sindie, we've got to talk because—"

She shushed him with an impatient wave of her hand, then emphatically tapped the window glass. "*Look!*"

Micah stared at her a moment longer before taking a look out the window. The desire to somehow make her see reason was still strong inside him, but already he could feel his resolve starting to crumble. As usual, he was overwhelmed by the sheer force of her personality.

He looked outside and saw two women standing on the sidewalk in front of the building. One was a woman named Tanya Connor. She was a moderately attractive blonde in her late twenties who lived in the bottom floor apartment facing the parking lot in building G. The other woman was one Micah was sure he'd never seen before, but he noted a bit of familial resemblance. He had a hunch she was Tanya's slightly older sister.

Sindie nudged him with an elbow. "Do you *see* that?"

Micah felt another faint twinge of nausea as he reluctantly nodded. "Uh … yeah."

After talking a few moments longer, the women on the sidewalk embraced warmly, then the one Micah didn't know got in a blue sedan parked at the curb and drove away. Tanya waved as she watched the woman who was probably her sister weave her way through the complex and finally disappear from sight.

Then she went back into her apartment.

Micah continued staring through the window even after he could no longer see the woman. He was barely aware of it when Sindie moved away from him and went into the kitchen. Tanya had looked the same as always except for one important detail—every visible inch of her skin was imbued with a sparkly shimmer of light.

His mind again flashed back to the night before. Speaking through his vessel, the priestess, the thing that was apparently Satan himself told the congregation they would gain the ability to identify the virginal by sight after consuming the blood and flesh of that night's sacrificial victim. This now appeared to have been the absolute truth. In light of what he knew and had experienced, there could be no other explanation for what he'd just seen. It hadn't been some weird optical illusion or trick of the light. The shimmer had been absent from the bare parts of the other woman's skin. The contrast when they'd embraced had been striking.

The revelation that Tanya had lived a sex-free life well into adulthood wasn't quite as shocking as that, but it did come as a bit of a surprise. She was decent-looking and had a nice body. He didn't get any kind of weird or off-putting vibe from her. Her sexless life was almost certainly a conscious choice rather than a result of being undesirable. Perhaps she was asexual. That was another of those previously marginalized communities he'd been hearing a bit more about lately.

The creak of a door opening finally diverted Micah's attention from the empty sidewalk. He turned his head in time to see Sindie leaving their apartment with a big butcher knife clutched in her right hand.

Oh, shit.

Micah ran after her, leaving the door to their apartment wide open. Buildings G and H were connected by a breezeway. The bare skin of his torso prickled in the chilly fall air as his feet pounded the stairwell steps between the buildings. His heart hammered painfully hard in his chest as his fear of what was about to happen rapidly mounted.

By the time he finally reached the first floor, the door to Tanya's apartment was coming open. Sindie was standing in front of it with the knife held behind her back. She glanced his way with a smirk and a wink. Tanya appeared in the doorway with a confused look on her face. She'd exchanged the clothes she'd been wearing for a plush pink bathrobe. Micah guessed she'd been on the verge of taking a shower when she'd heard the knock on her door.

"Sindie, don't!"

Tanya glanced briefly in his direction before focusing on Sindie. "Sindie? What's up? Do you need something?"

Sindie smiled. "As a matter of fact, I do, you virgin cunt. I need to kill you and take your pure fucking soul."

The look on Tanya's face conveyed utter shock and confusion. She had always known Sindie as the quirky but friendly girl who lived upstairs, a good, respectable neighbor who never made too much noise or caused trouble. Now that same nice girl was threatening to kill her for no good or obvious reason. The shock of it was so extreme it rendered her temporarily incapable of reacting or defending herself.

Sindie grabbed the woman by the throat and pushed her into the apartment. Micah hurried in after them, thinking he'd wrestle the knife away, but he was already too late.

Tanya was flat on her back on the living room floor. Sindie pulled open the front of her bathrobe and plunged the big, heavy blade deep into the quivering flesh of her abdomen. As Micah stood there and watched helplessly, she took the blade out and slammed it down again, punching another big hole in her stomach, which was already smeared bright red with blood. In between sobbing and squealing pitifully in pain, Tanya begged for mercy.

Sindie sneered. "Shut up, bitch. Satan is your master now."

She cut the woman's throat open and leaned over to let the spurting blood from the severed carotid splash against her face. When the blood flow slowed, she put her mouth to Tanya's throat and sucked more blood out through the big gash in her flesh.

Micah felt paralyzed, incapable of any kind of action.

Sindie made a slurping sound as she lifted her face from the dead woman's throat and turned her head to look at him. "Close the fucking door, bitch!"

Micah gaped at her in flabbergasted disbelief a moment longer. Then he swallowed hard and nodded. He went to the door and pushed it shut with trembling fingers. Successfully turning the lock required multiple attempts. When it was done, he put his back to the door and slid slowly to the floor, putting his face in his hands.

FIVE

Three years out of high school and Johnny Romero was still working at the goddamn Kwik Stop on the edge of town, out near the interstate junction. Most of the convenience store's customers were either hicks from the trailer park down the road or strangers passing through on their way to somewhere else. The ones passing through would pull in from the interstate to gas up and take a quick bathroom break, maybe grab some snacks while they were at it. The dumb hicks mostly came in to buy cheap beer and lottery tickets. Johnny had a little side business going with the younger trailer park denizens, selling them weak ragweed for about double what it was really worth, which wasn't much.

Once upon a time, he'd had bigger aspirations, imagining a

future in which he would get out of this nowhere town and make something of himself in the big city. The riddle he was never quite able to solve was exactly how he would go about doing that. He was only middling smart and had just managed to squeak by in high school. College was never a real option. Even if his grades had been more up to par, his dirt-poor, no-good parents wouldn't have been able to pay for a higher education for their only son. They didn't give a shit about him anyway, saving all their love and attention for his younger sister. She graduated high school two years after he did and now she was living in the next county over and going to that fancy-ass community college there. He hated that bitch. She thought she was better than him. He'd show her someday. Somehow.

The bell above the door chimed and a long-legged young woman in a yellow tube top and denim cutoffs came into the Kwik Stop. She was pretty, but her face had that hard-edged look to it that pegged her as one of the trailer park people. Or maybe not. After three years manning the counter here, he knew most of the local rednecks by sight, but he didn't think he'd ever seen this gal before. You could find a trailer park just about anywhere you went in this part of the country. Hell, maybe anywhere in the country, for all he knew. He wasn't exactly widely traveled. He'd never even left the state. So this gal was a redneck, but maybe she was a redneck from somewhere else.

He didn't know.

What he did know was her ass looked amazing in those tight cutoffs. He licked his lips and watched the way her buttocks moved as she walked down the middle aisle toward the bathrooms in the back. When he saw her go into the women's room and close the door, he stepped away from the counter and headed for the open door next to the cigarette racks behind the counter. Through this door was the cramped manager's office. Inside the office was a dented old metal desk and a filing cabinet that didn't see a lot of use in this digital age. The desk was pushed up against the wall in a corner of the room. On its surface was a laptop computer that dated from the latter stages of Bush 43's administration. It ran slower than molasses. In part that was due to its age, but another factor was all the viruses on it from the avalanche of porn he'd downloaded to it over the years.

Above the desk on a metal shelf bolted to the concrete wall was a row of color monitors. Using the keypad on the laptop, he was able to toggle through views from several angles inside and outside the store. In most ways, it was a pretty ordinary security setup. It did, however, feature one special extra bit of functionality that wasn't strictly legal. He hit some keys and the view on the middle monitor switched from the beer coolers to a shot of the hot number that had just waltzed into the women's bathroom.

The bathrooms here were the one-person-at-a-time type. There were no stalls, which meant nothing to obstruct his view. A couple years back, Johnny used some of his own money to buy and install a micro camera in the ladies' room. The camera had Bluetooth capability, which allowed him to patch it into the system here. Any time any reasonably good-looking chick came in to take a squirt or a shit while business was slow, he would slip into the office and check her out on the monitor, often getting a pretty good look at cooter or bare ass. Now and then, if the gal stayed in there long enough, he'd even get to rub one out. The monitor with a view of the parking lot allowed him to keep an eye out in case a customer showed up while he was beating off. He had all his bases covered.

In no way did Johnny feel bad about any of this. Holy hell would be raised if what he was doing ever became public knowledge, but he was relatively certain that would never happen. The well-hidden micro camera wasn't something anyone would ever notice. They'd have to actively be searching for it, which was unlikely. Besides all that, he believed he was owed a little something from the female of the species.

For as long as he could remember, girls had treated him like some kind of pariah, giving him dirty looks if he came near them or even looked their way. God forbid he should dare to speak to them, even if it was to say something nice, like how pretty their hair looked or how much he liked the dress they were wearing. In high school, he'd taken his share of beatings from angry boyfriends over that kind of thing. The worst beating he ever took, though, came at the hands of a trio of pissed-off girls after they caught him peeking in at the girls' locker room after gym class. They waited for him after school, forced him into a car with a stun device, and drove out to the middle of nowhere, where they dragged him out of the car and took turns punching and kicking the shit out of him until he couldn't move. They drove away, leaving him a bloody mess on the side of the road.

He'd held the incident against the so-called fairer sex ever since that day. His anger against women never came close to leading him down the path of becoming a serial killer. He knew some people saw him as a creep, but he wasn't *that* kind of creep. Not a killer. He was just a misunderstood guy who'd never gotten any poon because chicks had been mean to him his whole life. Came a point where he realized no babe would ever willingly have sex with him, which meant he had to take whatever meager level of pleasure he could by the limited means available to him.

The bitches *owed* him, dammit.

A little harmless voyeurism never hurt anybody anyway. It was a goddamn victimless crime is what it was. Hell, it was hardly a crime at all. More like a … whatchacallit … a *quirk*.

The leggy tube top gal spent some time fixing her lipstick at the sink, leaning over it and making kissy faces at the cracked and dirty mirror. Johnny hit a key and zoomed in for a closer look at her boobs. They were big ones and looked totally fucking awesome in that skintight top. When she was finished doing the lipstick thing, she stood up straight and looked at the mirror, tossing her hair and making the kissy face again. Then she grabbed her boobs and adjusted them in the top. Johnny groaned and squeezed his stiffening rod through his jeans. He zoomed back out when she went over to the toilet.

He let out a breath and squeezed his crotch harder. "Okay, baby, time for the main event."

The gal tore off strips of toilet paper and used them to cover the seat. He'd seen a lot of them do that. It was hilarious to him how afraid of germs or cooties they were. Heck, he cleaned the damn thing once a week every week without fail. When the seat was thoroughly covered, she lowered the cutoffs and her panties and gingerly sat down.

Johnny pulled at the tab of his zipper, sliding it down a few inches. He'd gotten a good, long look at this girl's shaved cooter. A longer than usual look thanks to her prissy reluctance to sit on the seat. The stimulation was more than he could take. He glanced at the parking lot monitor. Just two cars in the lot, his rust-bucket AMC Gremlin and a red Corvette he assumed belonged to the tube top gal.

Go for it.

He finished opening his pants and took out his dick. Before he started beating his meat in earnest, he pulled the box of tissues on the desk closer. When he looked at the monitor again, his breath caught in his throat and a chill slithered down his spine.

The gal was looking right at the spot in the corner of the bathroom where he'd installed the micro camera. On the other side of that wall was the room where they stored the extra beer. It was right behind the beer coolers. He'd stood on a ladder and drilled through the wall from there. It'd been easy. The sly, smirking look on her face suggested she knew the camera was there, but that wasn't possible. He'd never told anyone about it and it was practically invisible. The only thing he could guess was someone had come into the store and peeked into the office at a time when he'd been especially distracted, catching him in the act of spanking it while watching whatever gal had been in the bathroom at the time. He had a hard time believing he'd ever let his guard down enough for that to happen, but what other explanation could there be? The other thing he couldn't understand was why, if such a thing had happened, it hadn't been reported to the authorities.

Before he could spend any additional time thinking about it, however, something else strange happened.

The tube top gal leaned back, spread her legs, and reached between her legs. She tilted her head back and her mouth opened wide. He heard her moan softly and realized she was masturbating. He couldn't believe it. Nothing quite like this had ever happened at the Kwik Stop. A couple times redneck couples had slipped into the bathroom for a quick fuck, all the while believing they were being so sneaky, never realizing he knew what they were up to the whole time. Could see every second of it in HD video, even. But this was different. This wasn't some white trash piece of shit hooking up with some flabby redneck dude. This chick was *quality*. She had one of the sexiest bodies he'd ever seen. And more than that, she gave every indication of *performing* for him. She looked at the camera again and smiled, licking her lips.

Holy shit, Johnny thought. *She's fucking into it!*

Johnny's nostrils flared as he stared at the bathroom monitor and started stroking his cock harder and harder. He was on the verge of spraying jizz all over the desk when he heard the creak of the door opening wider behind him. Hurriedly tucking his junk away, he tapped a key to kill the bathroom feed. He then spun around on the swivel chair and saw that another hot chick had come into the Kwik Stop. This one was also a tall, leggy blonde, but her features were softer, less severe-looking, than those of the gal currently petting her cooter in the bathroom.

There was also something subtly familiar about the smugly superior look on her face.

Johnny frowned. "Do I know you?"

She laughed softly. "Sort of. Not really."

"What's that?"

He nodded at the Mason jar clasped securely in her elegant right hand. It contained some kind of clear liquid.

"A gift for you. Hail Satan, loser."

She came a step further into the room and splashed the contents of the jar against his face. He screamed as the powerful acid began to sizzle and melt his skin almost instantly, falling out of the chair and tumbling to his back on the dirty floor. Soon his eyes were burning, too, but before his vision went away entirely, he got a last blurry look at the gal who'd disfigured and blinded him. Tube top gal was standing next to her by then. They laughed at the sounds of his misery and started kicking him as he squirmed around on the floor.

Recognition came to him then. The second one was right. They didn't know each other. Not really. But he knew who they were, all right. These gals were two of the trio who'd administered that savage beating back in high school. They had returned to finish the job. When the knife pierced his heart, it felt almost like an act of mercy.

SIX

The all-day horror marathon on Channel 39 started at noon with an airing of *Night of the Living Dead.* Libby Nicholson, a sixteen-year-old junior year student at Littleburg High, skipped out of school early that day with the intention of watching the entire marathon from the beginning. She made it home just in time to pop a bag of microwave popcorn and get settled in on the couch in the den as the movie was starting.

Channel 39 was a local independent station, which meant the movies in the marathon would be edited for content. Profane language would be bleeped out and some of the nastier gore bits would be excised. This didn't bother Libby, who'd seen all the movies scheduled for the marathon in uncensored form countless times. Her father had a large DVD horror collection and many of the old gory classics were readily available on Shudder and numerous other streaming services. Broadcast television wasn't the only game in town anymore and hadn't been for a long time. These days you didn't have to watch a movie or show at a certain appointed time. VOD and streaming had changed everything. You could watch pretty much whatever you wanted whenever you wanted to watch it.

What VOD and the streaming services couldn't duplicate, for the most part, was the charm of seeing these movies hosted by Count Victor von Gravemore on *Shock Theater*. The hammy old performer had been hosting the weekly horror show on Channel 39 for decades and the annual all-day marathon was something Libby had looked forward to with great anticipation every year since elementary school.

She grabbed a handful of popcorn from the bowl in her lap and gobbled it down as she watched Gravemore mince his way around his set, which was designed to look like a vampire's lair in an old Hammer film. The wall behind him was covered with Styrofoam molded and painted to resemble the wall of a medieval dungeon. A casket with a plush red interior sat open on a long table. Dusty cobwebs were everywhere. An obviously fake severed head with wildly unkempt hair rested inside a wrought-iron birdcage dangling from the ceiling. Spooky sound effects played in the background. It was all so gloriously cheesy.

Gravemore delivered one of his trademark macabre puns, making Libby giggle as his segment ended and the movie resumed. She munched down another handful of popcorn and licked her fingers. The popcorn she favored was Butter Explosion. It was the most buttery popcorn available from the local grocery store and, in her opinion, the closest thing to real movie theater popcorn on the market. She sometimes consumed multiple bags of it over the course of a single night of watching movies. It was a wonder she hadn't gotten fat yet. Her first bowl of the marathon was almost empty already. She was debating whether to start popping a second bag when the doorbell rang.

Libby sighed.

Finally.

She set the bowl on the coffee table and got up to answer the door. The person out there on the porch was probably Anne Calloway. Anne's family had moved to Littleburg over the summer. Libby and Anne met at the start of the school year and quickly bonded over their mutual love of horror movies. She probably counted as Libby's closest friend at this point, which was pathetic in a way. She'd lived her whole life in this crappy town without ever forming any close friendships. Not that she spent too much time feeling all angsty over it. Most kids who grew up around here were basic in the blandest, dullest way. They were incapable of understanding someone like her. Anne, on the other hand, came from a bigger city and was more sophisticated. They could have philosophical conversations about life and the universe, something that had never been possible with the simple kids born and raised here. It'd been such an intellectually liberating thing for Libby. Such a total revelation.

What the other girl didn't know yet, however, was that Libby had developed a terrible crush on her. The crush had started out in a relatively light and innocent way in the earliest days of their friendship, but over time it'd become an obsession. She would lie awake in bed most nights and fantasize about making out with her friend, maybe even doing other things. Things Libby had never done before, not with anyone. When they were together, she burned with the need to tell Anne how she felt, but thus far she hadn't been able to work up the courage.

Maybe today would be the day. She had the house to herself. Her parents were at their jobs and wouldn't return home until early evening. There might never be a better time to make the kind of bold move she'd been yearning to make for weeks. No one would be around to cast judgment on her or interrupt. And if things worked out the way she hoped, the assurance of privacy might help Anne feel comfortable about doing some experimenting.

The last time they talked, Anne had promised to skip out as soon as she could and come over to watch the marathon with her. She had also promised to text Libby when she was on her way, but that hadn't happened yet. Maybe she'd just forgotten. It wouldn't be the first time.

Libby climbed the steps to the kitchen and passed through an archway into the foyer. The front door was about ten feet in front of her. She had a spring in her step and a smile on her face as she went quickly to the door, feeling more anxious than ever to see her new favorite person in the world. Her hand was already on the doorknob when a cautionary thought floated up from the depths of her mind. She still thought this was probably her friend on the other side of the door, but what if she was wrong?

Anne still hadn't texted her, after all. It was possible she was still in school and hadn't been able to slip away. Her morbid imagination made it too easy to believe some neighborhood creep had noticed her coming home early and had decided to come over and harass her. Or some random creep passing through had noticed the same thing and had also taken note of the absence of any other cars in the driveway. The latter seemed unlikely. The neighborhood was pretty quiet when she got home. She was sure she would have noticed any cars passing by in the street on her way into the house. Still, it couldn't hurt to be careful. She was a young girl alone at home at a time when most adults in the neighborhood were at work.

She took her hand away from the doorknob and raised up on her toes to peek through the peephole. When she saw who was on the porch, she experienced simultaneous feelings of relief and disappointment. The giddiness she'd been feeling at the prospect of seeing Anne evaporated. She wasn't out there. Instead, it was their neighbor from across the street, old Mr. Carson. He wasn't who she wanted to see, but he was nobody to fear. The elderly widower was kindly and harmless. She'd known him most of her life. He was standing too close to the door to see much other than his face. Up close like this, his eyes looked weird and googly behind his thick glasses.

While she wasn't afraid of the man, Libby didn't feel like

dealing with him. Ever since his wife died a few years back, he'd become a touch clingy with his neighbors. Conversations that should have been finished inside of a few minutes at most often dragged on for thirty or forty minutes. Sometimes longer. Libby felt sorry for him. He was clearly lonely and desperate for inter- action with other people. That was undeniably sad. It also wasn't her problem. She didn't want him to be here when Anne finally showed up, which should be soon.

Ignoring him seemed like the best way to go. He obviously knew she was home. The car in the driveway was an unavoidable dead giveaway. That being the case, not opening the door to see what he wanted could be construed as a tad rude. Then again, she was under no obligation to speak to this man. She didn't want to risk missing an hour of the Channel 39 marathon just to listen to him ramble on about inconsequential bullshit. If he asked about it later, she would tell him she hadn't heard the doorbell because she'd been upstairs taking a nap. He would probably mention her early return home to her parents, but she wasn't worried about that. She would just tell them she'd come home early because she wasn't feeling well. They never pressed her much about things like that. They knew she skipped on occa- sion, but she kept her grades at a high level, so it wasn't viewed as a real source of concern.

"I know you're in there, little Libby," Carson called out in his croaky old man's voice. "Can hear you breathing. Open up just a second, please. Got something pretty darn important to ask you. I won't keep you long, I promise."

Libby sighed heavily.

Her shoulders sagged in despondent surrender as she thought, *Might as well get this over with. I just hope I'm able to get back to the marathon before it's fucking over.*

She unlocked the door and pulled it open. "I'm kind of busy with something, Mr. Carson. What is it you—"

She stopped talking when she realized he was grinning at her in a weird way. The expression was unlike any she'd ever seen on his face. It was more of a leer than a normal grin. Something else was weird, too. He was holding something behind his back. Libby's hand tightened around the edge of the door. Her heart was racing as she began to realize her assessment of the old man as harmless might not have been entirely accurate. The urge to slam the door in his face and lock it again was strong.

He chuckled and the darkly malicious, unfriendly grin grew wider. "Hey there, girly. Got a little surprise for you."

He showed her what he'd been hiding behind his back.

Libby screamed.

Anne had worn her pretty blonde hair in pigtails today. Mr. Carson was holding her severed head by one of the pigtails. It was swaying back and forth in his grip. He must have killed her mere minutes ago, because blood was still dripping from her ragged neck stump.

Libby screamed again.

Mr. Carson laughed. "Catch, bitch."

He tossed Anne's head at her. Libby reached out and caught it instinctively, holding it no longer than a second before screaming yet again and letting go of it. Her dead friend's head landed on the tiled floor with a heavy thump. She knew she should act fast and get the door shut before the old maniac could come into the house, but her shock rooted her to the spot.

Carson leaned to his left and grabbed something he'd propped up in a corner of the small porch. When he came into the house, he was holding an axe with a long handle. The heavy axe head's blade looked wickedly sharp and was coated in blood.

The old man chuckled again in that oily, insidious way. "Satan wants your soul and I'm here to collect it. Get ready to die, virgin bitch."

Libby kept her eye on the axe as she started moving backward. He wasn't yet close enough to take a good swing at her, but that wouldn't last long if she didn't take serious evasive or defensive action soon. Her fear level was significant, but she had the advantage of being younger and faster than this elderly murderer. If she could just keep her wits about her and act swiftly, she could take herself out of harm's way and get to safety with relative ease.

Her keys were on the counter in the kitchen. All she had to do was run in there and grab them, then go out the side door to her car. Her phone was down in the den, but she would have to leave that behind. She could be gone from here in less than thirty seconds. No point in complicating things and increasing the risk to her life by going for something she didn't need.

Carson came a step closer and began to raise the axe.

Libby took another step backward.

Carson sneered. "You stay right where you are, missy. Time to take your medicine."

Libby was on the verge of turning around and running into the kitchen when she felt strong hands grab her by the shoulders from behind and hold her in place. She twisted her head around and was stunned to see the grinning face of her father. The shock of seeing him now, under these circumstances, was nearly as extreme as what she'd felt upon realizing her beautiful Anne had been murdered. Why was he grinning at her like that? Why was he keeping her from getting out of the way of that bloody axe? And why wasn't he still at work? She hadn't even heard him come into the house.

Her father, the man who'd never treated her with anything other than total affection and understanding, laughed at her confusion. "You're probably wondering why I'm home. I got a call from your school about you skipping out. Usually I ignore those calls, but not today. Today is special, you see."

Carson chuckled. "Damn right it is. Now hold the bitch still while I put the steel in her."

"Not so fast, Carson."

This was another voice. A female voice. Libby gasped in shock again as her mother brushed past her husband and came into the foyer. Her mother was an attractive middle-aged lady who looked several years younger than her actual age. She was wearing tight designer jeans and a white top with a low-scooped neckline. A pair of dark sunglasses dangled from the collar.

"By rights, this is our kill, Carson. She's our fucking daughter. Hand me the axe."

She extended a hand with her palm held upward.

Carson looked like he wanted to argue about it for a moment. Then his features sagged and he shook his head in disgust.

He handed her the axe.

Candice Nicholson turned toward her daughter and came a few steps closer. She then stopped and spread her feet apart in a stance similar to that of a baseball player standing inside a batter's box, smiling as she began to raise the axe.

"I'm sorry, sweetie. I do love you. But I love Satan more."

Libby trembled in terror in her father's unbreakable grip. Tears were streaming down her face. "Why are you doing this? I don't understand."

Her father put his mouth against her ear. "It's your fault, you know. This wouldn't be happening if you'd ever let some lucky boy fuck you."

Candice nodded, her expression mildly regretful. "He's right, you know. But it's too late for that now."

She raised the axe even higher, turned her hips, and began to swing it forward.

Libby wailed in despair one last time. *"Please don't kill me!"*

The heavy axe blade punched deep into her belly. The agony as the steel ripped through her organs was far beyond any level of pain she'd ever imagined. That pain doubled when her mother ripped the blade out again. Blood and pieces of shredded organs spilled out of the huge rent in her flesh. Her mother adjusted her grip on the axe and raised it again, this time high over her head.

KILL FOR SATAN!

When she brought it down for the second and last time, the blade cleaved through the top of Libby Nicholson's skull, killing her instantly.

SEVEN

Micah felt like he was living inside a nightmare. Hours had passed since he'd stood by helplessly while watching his beautiful but apparently deranged girlfriend savagely murder their downstairs neighbor, but it still felt like it'd happened only minutes ago. His mind kept replaying the image of Sindie sucking the blood from the dead woman's throat wound. She had looked truly demented then, like some kind of feral beast instead of a human being. Watching her do that had been horrifying enough, but then she insisted he drink blood, too.

He didn't want to do it, of course, but he had no choice. Not with the way she was acting. He feared her unleashing some of that murderous frenzy on him if he resisted. He didn't want to believe she would hurt him. She loved him. She said it dozens of times every day and he'd never once doubted the sincerity of the declarations, but she was unhinged right now. There was no telling what a person in that mental state might do, even to a loved one.

So he drank some of Tanya's blood. Way more of it than he would have liked. This was because Sindie kept urging him to have more and more. Which was bad enough, but she kept sinking to lower and lower depths of depravity. She used the butcher knife to cut off pieces of the dead woman's flesh, eating them raw and forcing Micah to do the same. He got violently sick after, but he did it.

After that, she dragged him into the shower in Tanya's apartment. The hot water sluiced away the blood and Sindie went down on him. Despite the stressful circumstances, her expert tongue had him painfully stiff within seconds. When he thought he was about to come, she got to her feet and had him fuck her from behind. The orgasm that came less than a minute later relieved some of his tension for a short time. That lasted until they went back out to the living room and she ordered him to piss on Tanya's corpse.

"Why?" he asked her with a horrified look on his face.

She sneered. "To revel in her total desecration. Why the fuck else? Do it, Micah."

He did what she wanted, of course, like always, and he didn't stop urinating all over the dead woman's face until he'd squeezed every last drop from his bladder. When he was finished, Sindie pulled him into a rough embrace and kissed him with a violent hunger.

"I love you, Micah," she told him, stealing a moment to catch a breath. "I love you so fucking much."

Her tongue was in his mouth again before he could respond in kind.

The time since then had passed in a haze. He was barely aware of what was happening as Sindie dragged him to various locations all over town. What he did know was she had killed at least one more person already that afternoon. There'd been a guy walking along the side of a road at some point during their travels. Micah never even glanced at him, only perceiving his presence as a vague shape at the edge of his vision. Then Sindie abruptly swerved her car toward the man and ran him down, jostling Micah in his seat as the tires bounced over the body. He never even saw whether the man's skin had that virgin shimmer and he didn't bother asking Sindie. She might have killed the man for the pure hell of it, for no reason other than she'd discovered she liked doing it.

Another time she parked outside an unfamiliar house in a nice middle-class neighborhood. She didn't say anything to him as she got out of the car and went up to the porch to ring the doorbell. The door opened a moment later and an older lady he didn't recognize came out onto the porch and hugged her. They then went inside the house. Sindie didn't reemerge for a while. His dazed state of mind made it difficult to gauge how much time passed, but he later figured she stayed in there at least a half-hour.

She didn't say anything about what happened in the house when she finally came back out to the car, but she had flecks of blood on her clothes and at the corners of her mouth. He didn't know for certain she'd killed anyone in there, but it seemed a safe bet. As with the pedestrian she'd run down, he had no clue why she would want to kill the older lady. He knew, however, that the woman's probable murder had nothing to do with the devil's decree. There'd been no hint of the virgin shimmer on her wrinkled old skin. The embrace Sindie shared with her on the porch suggested she'd been someone close to her. A relative. Maybe even her mother. Micah had no idea. Sindie didn't talk about her family and had never introduced him to any of them. So much about her life beyond being a Satanist and what she did for a living remained a total mystery to him.

Their next stop was a hardware store. Again, Micah remained in the car while his crazy girlfriend went in and took care of whatever business she was here to conduct. This time, though, the store's windows allowed him to observe her moving through the aisles. He was relieved to see she wasn't brutally murdering the store's employees. She made her purchases and came back out to the car in less than five minutes.

Now they were sitting in her Kia Sorento in the parking lot outside a Baptist church. It was about half past three in the afternoon.

Micah looked at Sindie and raised an eyebrow. "What are we doing here? And why did you buy machetes at the hardware store?"

Sindie cut the engine and removed her keys from the ignition. "The machetes are for killing virgins. Duh. Come on, Micah. You're not stupid. I would think you could figure that out. As for why we're here, there's two reasons. One is that at this very minute a meeting of the Youth Abstinence League of Littleburg is taking place in the basement of this building. Virgins galore. We're here to kill as many of them as possible, preferably all of them. As a bonus, my worthless, god-fearing little sister is one of them. Killing that bitch while she cowers and begs for mercy will be the highlight of my fucking day, I can tell you that right now."

Micah gaped at her in disbelief. "What? You really want to kill your sister?"

Sindie huffed in a disdainful way. "Yes."

"But … why?"

Her head snapped toward him, her pretty features twisted in a look of pure fury. "Because I fucking hate her. That's all you need to know."

"Did you kill that woman when you went into her house?"

"Yes."

"Was she your mother?"

"Yes."

Each time Sindie answered in the affirmative, it sounded like she was spitting out a tooth. It was clear she had a lot of pent-up negative feelings where her family was concerned. He wasn't sure whether mercilessly slaughtering them all was the healthiest way of expressing her feelings, but they were sort of past the point where an alternative path could have been pursued.

She let out a breath and her facial muscles began to relax, resuming their usual, softer appearance. "You're coming with me this time, Micah. No sitting back and letting me do all the dirty work. Get out of the fucking car."

She got out before he could say anything to that.

With great reluctance, Micah opened the door on his side and got out, too. She was standing at the back of the Sorento with the rear hatch open. By the time he joined her there, she had already removed the machetes. She handed one to Micah and closed the hatch.

She looked at him and said, "Are you ready?"

He shook his head. "Not really."

She scowled at him. "I don't get what the actual fuck your problem is. Last night at the mass it felt like you were as committed to all this as I am. Now, not so much. What happened?"

Micah shrugged. "Last night was just weird, okay? I wasn't myself. Not really. It was like I was under the influence of mind control drugs or something, like some outside force was fucking around in my head and making me feel things I wouldn't ordinarily feel."

"And today?"

Another shrug. "The drugs wore off and I feel like the real me again. And the real me is a regular guy who isn't much interested in randomly killing a bunch of people."

"Fuck what you want," Sindie said, showing him a disgusted look. "You're doing it anyway or you and me are over." She raised her machete and put the tip of the blade to his throat. "Permanently. You get me?"

Micah thought he did get her meaning. She was threatening his life without explicitly verbalizing it. Given how much she claimed to love him, it was the clearest and strongest evidence yet of the depth of her commitment to Satan.

He swallowed and managed a single nervous nod. "Yeah. I get you."

She huffed. "Good. Now come on."

She turned away from him and started striding rapidly in the direction of the church. He stayed where he was a moment longer, watching the sexy sway of her hips. She was still wearing the sleeveless Cradle of Filth shirt, but she'd changed out the cotton shorts for a pair of black vinyl hot pants. Imprinted across the backside of the hot pants was the word SATAN in large silver letters. Whatever else you could say about her, she wasn't exactly subtle about her Luciferic allegiances. And despite all the atrocities he'd watched her commit, he remained powerfully attracted to her.

Sindie stopped in her tracks and looked over her shoulder at him. "Goddammit, Micah. Get your ass in gear. You're not getting out of this."

Micah was on the horns of a dilemma here. He could make a run for it and try to get out of town, but that would come with the risk of being tracked down and killed by Sindie or one of the other Satanists. And one thing he knew from the two midnight masses he'd attended, there were a *lot* of Satanists in this little town. Like, a really shockingly high number of them. Escape seemed unlikely, for all the reasons that had kept him from trying it up to this point as well as some new ones.

There was only one real option.

Accept his fate as a servant of the devil and embrace doing the horrific things the dark lord commanded. If nothing else, it would make his girlfriend happy.

Fuck it.

He caught up with Sindie and together they went into the church.

EIGHT

The girls were already working on some of their routines when Felicity Harper parked her Toyota Highlander outside the practice field at the training facility adjacent to Littleburg High. She sat in the SUV and watched them for a few minutes while smoking a cigarette and listening to a breaking news bulletin on a local AM radio station. The announcer was talking in urgent tones about a "wave of violence" hitting Littleburg, with the station receiving numerous reports of seemingly unconnected murders and violent assaults happening all over town.

Littleburg was a small town, a fact that was literally right there in the name. Not desolate plains of Nebraska small, but small enough. Whole years went by—sometimes several in a row—without a single murder being reported. With more than a dozen confirmed victims so far—and reports of more coming in every few minutes—it wasn't hard to conclude that what was happening today wasn't some weird, anomalous blip. So far the victims were not linked in any obvious way, but some level of coordination among the perpetrators seemed likely.

The station played a clip of a brief statement from Sheriff Ron Carpenter: "If there's a pattern to it, I'll be damned if I know what it is, but we're working hard to contain things and keep our citizens safe. For now, my best advice is for everyone to stay inside and don't open your doors for anyone."

Felicity Harper turned off the radio and flicked her half-smoked cigarette out the window. She grabbed her backpack and got out of the Highlander, leaving the key in the ignition with the engine running. The practice field was surrounded by a chain-link fence. She opened a gate and stepped out onto the field. The gate remained open behind her.

The cheerleaders were assembled in the middle of the field, some twenty-five yards from where she'd entered through the gate. At the moment, they were rehearsing one of the more complex routines, with some of the girls standing on the shoulders of other girls beneath them. They were performing the routine with admirable skill and precision, without the slightest hint of a hiccup. She wanted to clap when she saw how smoothly the girls up top executed their dismount. This year's squad was as good or better than any she'd had during her eleven years as cheerleading coach at Littleburg High. It was a tribute to their athleticism and dedication to craft, but also a product of her leadership skills. She had a genuine gift for guiding the girls and getting the most from them.

Felicity took great pride in seeing this evidence of her talent, another indication of which was on display here today. In all her years as a cheerleading coach, she'd never once been late for a practice. She was always here well ahead of time, ready to greet and get started with the first girls to show up. That had changed today. She was more than thirty minutes late. She wasn't happy about it, but it had been unavoidable. Despite that, the girls were showing their commitment to greatness by starting practice without her. Another squad, a lazier one led by a less demanding coach, might have spent this time unproductively, perhaps staring at their phones or lounging around and gossiping with their squad mates. But not these girls.

Adrienne O'Bannon was this year's head cheerleader and a shoo-in to be named Homecoming Queen. Appropriately, she'd taken it upon herself to lead the squad through their routines in the absence of their coach. There were no ugly or even homely girls on the squad. Being pretty was an unwritten but understood requirement. Even so, Adrienne was on a level far above the rest of them. She was easily the most attractive young lady Felicity had ever coached.

Had fate taken a different course, many of these girls would have done well in life after graduation. Some might have moved on to greener pastures far from the constricting confines of conservative Littleburg, finding success in the corporate world or as tech innovators. They were that smart. Others would have stayed to start families and take on other traditional roles in the community, becoming local business leaders and politicians. A few others, inevitably, would have spiraled downward in the years after school, perhaps ending up as strippers at the Sin Den just outside the town line. Felicity had long pegged the squad's lesbian couple—Vicky Hooper and Layla Dozier—as prime candidates for that inglorious fate.

Adrienne was something else altogether. She was special, a rare, brilliant flower. She could do anything she wanted. Become a top research scientist, for instance, developing treatments for deadly diseases. Or go to Paris or New York and become a high fashion model. She had the cheekbones and build to become iconic in the latter field, but she also possessed the keen intellect necessary for the former. Unfortunately for her, she was also a virgin.

Felicity felt a touch of melancholy at seeing the girl's skin imbued with that sparkling shimmer. Before today, her virginal status wouldn't have mattered to anyone other than the many guys constantly trying to get into her pants, but now it was a death sentence. It was too bad. A waste, really. But this mild twinge of regret was easily shunted aside. It was a small thing compared to the love she felt for Satan.

She was a few yards away from the spot where the squad members were gathered when Adrienne greeted her with a warm and friendly smile. "Hello, Miss Harper! Hope you don't mind, but we took it on ourselves to get going today. We figured it was what you'd want."

Felicity smiled and knelt on the field in front of Adrienne, still carefully maintaining that distance of a few yards. She began to unzip the backpack. "You assume correctly, Adrienne. Very commendable."

She rooted around in the backpack a moment before taking out two Glock pistols, one in each hand. There were exclamations of surprise when the girls first saw the guns. These gave way to shouts of terror and confusion when she stood and aimed one of the guns at Adrienne and shot her through the center of the forehead. Screams rang out on the practice field as blood from the exit wound at the back of Adrienne's head splashed the uniforms of the cheerleaders standing directly behind her.

Most of the girls stood there in shock that first moment. The spell was broken by Layla Dozier, who was the first of them to make a run for it. She was standing at the rear of the squad with her girlfriend when that first shot shattered the afternoon calm. She was running in the opposite direction within seconds of Adrienne's corpse hitting the ground.

Felicity started firing rapidly with both pistols, swinging them about and picking off her targets with ruthless efficiency. She'd spent years practicing her marksmanship at shooting ranges. It was a hobby, a thing she did for fun. Nothing more than that. She never even thought of it in terms of practicing for home defense. She certainly never expected to utilize her shooting skill on live targets, but she was happy to use it now in service of Satan.

Except for Layla, none of the girls got very far after finally attempting to flee. She gunned them all down, even the ones who weren't virgins, which was most of them. Felicity had counted a total of five with the skin shimmer, all of whom were now dead. Five pure souls successfully collected for the glory of Satan. That made a total of seven for her on the day. She hoped to collect many more before midnight.

Layla was still running hard toward the opposite end of the practice field. There was another gate down there. Given a few more seconds of hard running, she'd be able to make it to the gate and then out to safety. It came as no surprise to Felicity that the girl's flesh didn't have the purity shimmer. She wondered about that as she sized up a shot, aiming one of the pistols at Layla's back.

For the devil's purposes, what exactly constituted a loss of virginity? Did it require the penetration of a vagina by a penis or did same-sex sexual activity also remove the shimmer? She already knew the shimmer only became visible on the skin of persons who'd reached the stage of sexual maturity, which eliminated the necessity of killing small children. Though she was a thoroughly committed Satanist, she was kind of grateful for that. This other matter struck her as a gray area, though. If nothing else, it would make for an interesting discussion topic at the next midnight mass.

Accuracy could be a tricky thing with a handgun at this distance, but if there was anyone who could bring the little lezzie down from here, it was Felicity. She waited one more second and then, just as Layla was about to open the gate, she squeezed the trigger.

The gun clicked empty.

Felicity scowled at it.

Shit.

She tried to bring the other gun to bear on the fleeing teenager, but by then Layla had the gate open and was running through it.

It was too late.

She grabbed her backpack and stowed the pistols inside it again. After zipping it up, she walked at an unhurried pace back out to the parking lot. While she wished she'd been able to finish off the last member of her varsity squad, it wasn't that big a deal. Killing the girls who weren't virgins hadn't strictly been necessary, but she figured Satan would appreciate her taking any innocent life. The virgin souls might earn her more infernal credit or whatever, but there had to be at least a little value in the rest of them. If not, so what? She still had lots of ammo and many hours to go before midnight.

She also wasn't worried about letting a witness to her crime escape. There were undoubtedly other witnesses cowering behind the bleachers or inside the weight-training building. It didn't matter if anyone had seen her gun down the cheerleaders because the cult was well-entrenched at the highest levels of power in Littleburg. Any potential witnesses who tried to come forward after today would be silenced. The whole thing would be swept under the rug and life here would go back to something resembling normal.

As if none of this had even happened.

NINE

This Wednesday's YALL meeting was even lamer than usual. Seth wouldn't have thought such a thing possible, but it was true. The Wednesday meetings were always so tedious and uncomfortable. On some Sundays, upwards of fifty kids crowded into this basement. On days like that, he could blend into the background and not have to work too hard at pretending he wanted to be here. He could retreat into his own mind and tune out the religious brainwashing bullshit. Time passed fast on those days, which was also nice.

The Wednesday meetings were more sparsely attended. Usually only twenty or so kids showed up, which meant he wasn't always able to fade into the background and was sometimes forced to participate in group discussion. He blushed a lot and stammered when he had to speak in front of other YALL members, some of whom actually were good little Christian kids. Some of his difficulty could be chalked up to a natural aversion to public speaking. Whatever his future held, he knew for an absolute fact it wouldn't involve being a lecturer or politician. Any kind of spotlight was not something he craved. Another factor, perhaps an even bigger one, was how talking in group required him to blatantly lie about how hard he was working not to give in to sinful temptations. Seth was all in favor of giving in to temptation. He was in favor of sin in general. The fun ones, anyway. Given half a chance, he would surrender to temptation in the tiniest measurable fraction of a second possible.

The lying didn't come easily because if he couldn't make himself believe the bullshit coming out of his mouth, how could he possibly convince anyone else? At least he was usually only required to speak a couple minutes at a time. Minutes that seemed like hours. Today's meeting was worse than usual, though, because attendance was at an all-time low. Including himself, only nine kids were at the meeting. That meant he'd have to talk more.

He was feeling intensely anxious about that as the official start time for the meeting drew near without the usual trickle of late arrivals showing up. The nine of them really were going to be the only ones here. He wished he could just leave, but his dad would find out and then there'd be holy hell to pay. Nope, he was stuck here, as always, whether he liked it or not.

A few group members retrieved some of the folding chairs

stowed at the back of the basement and arranged them in a loose circle in the middle of the room. The circle was markedly smaller than usual. Seth would be much closer to the kids on the opposite side of the circle when it was his time to speak. Just thinking about the closer proximity of those faces made his armpits damp.

Something curious was going on, though, a weird vibe in the room he couldn't quite figure out. Most other members of the group were fixated on their phones, which were usually turned off and stowed away at this point. Some of them were muttering and frantically texting away. Caitlin Winthrop was off in a corner by herself doing just that. He could see her mouthing curses. He lip-read some serious bits of profanity, the likes of which he'd never heard pass through her lips. It made him miss his confiscated phone more than ever.

He was trying to work up the nerve to ask someone—maybe even Caitlin—what was going on when the door to the basement in the far corner of the room burst open and two black-clad individuals came running in. Both looked like they were in their early twenties. The guy was tall and lanky with curly black hair to his shoulders. His female companion was in tiny hot pants and a sleeveless Cradle of Filth shirt. She was gorgeous and something in her facial features was vaguely familiar. Judging from the look of murderous rage on her face, though, he figured there was a high likelihood she was completely insane. Or pretending to be.

She raised the machete over her shoulder and screamed at the members of YALL: *"Time to die for Satan, virgin bitches!"*

Seth frowned.

Uh … this is pretty weird. What the fuck is going on?

His first thought was these two were playing some kind of twisted Halloween prank. It was just too obvious. Running into a meeting of a youth abstinence group and waving machetes around on Halloween seemed like exactly the kind of thing people heavily into black metal—as he assumed these two were based on that Cradle of Filth shirt and their general look— would find hilarious. They would probably take some play swipes at some of the group members with their rubber machetes, scaring the hell out of them before running out again. He had to admit it actually was kind of funny. A little smile had even formed at the edges of his mouth. Funnily enough, though, no one else in the group seemed even slightly amused. Some even looked … scared?

Seth's frown deepened.

Huh.

Steve Combs tentatively approached the girl with his hands held outward in a placating gesture. Combs was a member of the Littleburg High football team. He was tall and had a solid linebacker's build. It was hard to imagine a guy like Combs being afraid of a slightly built girl wielding a rubber machete, but his tentative demeanor suggested some real concern.

"Look, we don't want any trouble here," he told her, keeping his hands extended in what Seth now saw as a defensive or warding-off gesture. "You need to get out of here before I take that machete and—"

The girl screamed and swung the machete down, the blade

slicing through Combs's flesh and bone with shocking ease and taking his hand off at the wrist. Blood jetted from his wrist stump, splashing against the front of the girl's Cradle of Filth shirt. The basement filled with screams. Combs screamed and gripped his wrist stump with his good hand as more blood continued to spurt out of it. The girl swung the machete again and this time it chopped deeply into the side of Steve's neck. When she yanked the blade free of his flesh, more blood spurted from a severed artery. His head lolled to one side and in another moment he toppled over, a wide pool of blood spreading out around his head on the floor.

Another of the guys in the group let out a defiant scream and took a run straight at the Cradle of Filth girl. He'd picked up one of the folding chairs and apparently meant to swing it at her. Before he could do that, though, the crazy girl's companion stepped forward and swung his machete. It split the face of the group's would-be defender right through the middle, stopping him cold. The tall guy ripped his machete free and swung it around a second time. This time the blade chopped through the group member's neck, taking his head off his shoulders as easily as it'd cut down a cornstalk. A geyser of blood erupted from the neck stump as the severed head tumbled to the floor and rolled.

More screaming ensued. Seth realized he was screaming by then, too. Any notion of this violent attack being a funny Halloween prank was gone. That had ended the instant the girl's machete took off Steve's hand. Aside from the occasional beatings dished out by his piece-of-shit father, he'd never seen scary real-life violence up close like this. Real danger—potentially mortal danger—was right in front of him.

The world was spinning. He felt dizzy, like he might fall over any second now, which would probably be a death sentence. He didn't know what to do. The only way out of the basement was through the door the machete-wielding maniacs had just burst through. And they were still effectively blocking the way. Any chance of escape would require psyching up his nerve to run right past them. He wasn't sure he could do that, even if inaction spelled his doom. His fear was that overpowering.

So that's what you're gonna do, huh? he asked himself. *Just lie down and be killed?*

It appeared so. He glanced to his left and saw Caitlin. Like him, she was standing with her back pressed to the wall. She was only a few feet away from him. He wanted to reach out and grip her hand for comfort. Even now, though, facing almost certain death at the hands of these psychos, she would probably jerk her hand away, shunning physical contact with the pathetic geek.

The machete-wielders came deeper into the room. At the girl's direction, they spread out some to reduce the chance of any group members running around them and getting to the door. A female member of the group had tripped over her own feet in her attempt to retreat and was on her back on the floor. She was trying to scramble backward as the attackers came closer, but she kept slipping and sliding in a big pool of blood. The female attacker caught up to her and stood over her a moment before shoving the machete blade deep into her belly. This triggered more screaming mixed in with some sobs from the surviving group members, all of whom would also soon be dead at this rate.

Then the crazy girl spotted Caitlin cowering in the corner and did a thing Seth found odd even in this already bizarre and highly fucked-up context. She smiled. Then she began to laugh. Caitlin shook her head and began to mutter the word "no" over and over.

The crazy girl's smile faded and gave way to a sneering look of explosive fury. A second later, she raised the machete and came charging straight at Caitlin. Seth spent a paralyzed instant watching her rush forward. Then he took a panicked look around and spied the closed door to the supply closet a dozen feet to his right.

You better be unlocked, motherfucker.

He grabbed Caitlin by the hand and hauled her in that direction with all his might.

TEN

The third movie in Channel 39's all-day horror marathon was *Motel Hell*. With commercials added in and a few small bits of potentially offensive content edited out, its television run-time was two hours, same as all the other movies in the marathon. Regardless of the original run-times of the theatrical versions, whether they clocked in at eighty minutes or two and a half hours, all were either cut down or extended via a combination of extra commercials and longer host segments to fit a two-hour slot.

The next movie in the marathon's schedule was *Videodrome*, one of Wesley Campbell's all-time favorites. It'd be interesting to see how badly the hacks at Channel 39 butchered David Cronenberg's early '80s masterpiece. He suspected it would be barely recognizable, with all the fantastic transgressive elements scrubbed away. Which begged the question—why even attempt to pare down a film like *Videodrome* to the point of being palatable to a broadcast television audience if by doing so you were robbing it of its true essence?

All things considered, Wesley thought the movie a distinctly odd choice to show the predominantly mainstream audience watching the marathon. Most of them would have only a casual interest in horror at best. The sort of people who only became interested in spooky movies when the calendar flipped over to October. Even then, the casuals mainly only wanted to see a limited range of standard genre offerings. Various installments of the *Halloween* and *Friday the 13th* franchises. Stephen King adaptations. That sort of thing. Wesley was no genre snob. He loved those movies as much as he loved films that were more daring and experimental. They were pure fun. Nothing wrong with that.

At about the midpoint of *Motel Hell*, Channel 39 cut away from the movie to a Count Gravemore host segment. Cheesy organ music swelled as the count cackled in a faux-demented way. The camera zoomed in on the count's makeup-covered face as he began to describe his own failed attempt to cultivate a human garden. He went on to explain how it didn't work because of the "rot" in the Transylvanian soil. A lot of the count's segments were like that, taking inspiration from the movies he was hosting. He'd weave in a lot of corny jokes and macabre puns, most of them so bad they would've made Forry Ackerman cringe. The actor playing the count was the hammiest performer Wesley had ever seen. He delivered his lines in a way that made him seem like a discount Vincent Price.

Wesley thought the guy was completely awesome. He hoped the man would live forever and keep hosting movies on Channel 39 until the end of time. This was unlikely, of course, but the prospect of a world without the Count and his cheesy show was a staggeringly dreary thing to contemplate.

When the segment ended and the station went to commercial, Wesley got up to go to the bathroom. He was up to five beers and it was still relatively early. Trips to the bathroom to unburden his bladder were becoming more frequent and it would only get worse as the dead soldiers continued to pile up on the coffee table. Any other day he would not be slamming back the brewskies this early, but today was Halloween, his favorite day of the year. For Wesley, it'd always been a day to celebrate, even if he mostly had to celebrate alone. It was the one day of the year when the rest of society wholeheartedly embraced the genre that'd fascinated him most of his life. The one day when the world made sense and he didn't feel like an ill-fitting puzzle piece. An emotional crash would come tomorrow, but for now he wasn't thinking about that.

After leaving the bathroom, he went into the kitchen to grab another beer from the fridge. He was just pulling the door open when he heard a crash from the vicinity of the back yard. Frowning, he went into the adjacent dining room to peer out at the yard through the big window there. He pulled back the gauzy curtain and took a look around. His frown deepened. No one was out there, unless they were hiding in the old shed at the back of the yard. Also out there was a small wooden deck accessible via the door in the kitchen. The red BBQ grill on the deck was tipped over on its side. He figured that was the source of the crash he'd heard, but he wasn't sure what might have caused it to happen. The grill was of sturdy construction. Knocking it over would require something considerably more jarring than a stiff breeze. He took another look around the big yard, his heart beating faster at the unnerving thought that some intruder might have attempted to enter the house.

He went back into the kitchen for a look out the French door that opened onto the deck. His heart rate quickened again when he noticed the position of some of the lounge chairs, which appeared to have been shoved aside. Someone—or something—had definitely been out there on the deck within the last few minutes. The grill toppling over was one thing. If he'd tried hard enough, he could've come up with a non-sinister explanation for that. When taken in context with the changed position of the chairs, that wasn't really possible.

Could an animal have done this?

He wasn't sure.

A dense stand of trees stood beyond the fenced-in back yards on this side of the street. There was some fairly active wildlife out there. Try as he might, though, he couldn't imagine some big animal coming out of the woods to hop over the chain-link fence and come up onto the deck. This was his parents' house.

He was housesitting for them while they were on vacation in Costa Rica. When he'd lived here as a kid, he never once saw a forest creature of any significant size in the yard. Sometimes he saw possums and squirrels, but that was about it.

No.

An animal hadn't done this. There was no point in trying to explain away the disarray on the deck. A human being had done this. Probably one with some level of ill intent. It was common knowledge among their neighbors and friends that Bob and Pamela Campbell were out of town for an extended period. Some shady piece of shit criminal type might easily have become aware of their absence. What he'd heard might well have been a would-be burglar trying to get into the house, one who'd gotten spooked and run away after detecting unexpected sounds of human activity inside.

Wesley shuddered at the thought, which was more than a little creepy. Despite feeling creeped out, he was sure he had nothing to worry about. The intruder was gone and almost certainly wouldn't be returning now that he knew the house was occupied. He could probably safely put it out of his head and go back to the horror marathon now. Still, he hesitated, wondering whether he should call the police to file a report. He rejected the idea when he pictured how the macho cops responding to the call would smirk when he told them what he suspected and pointed to the slight level of disarray on the deck as his only evidence. A smirk that would say, *That's what you called us out here for? You're a little pussy, aren't you?*

Wesley sighed.

Nope. Definitely not calling the cops.

He decided he would grab another beer and get back to the marathon, but first he would go out on the deck and put things back in order. The intruder had scampered away and was no longer a threat. It was still daylight out for a little longer. There was nothing to worry about.

The door's hinges squealed slightly as he pulled it open and stepped out onto the deck. It'd been warmer earlier in the day, but the air had that chilly fall bite to it now. He was wearing only a short-sleeved t-shirt and cotton gym shorts. Goosebumps rose on his exposed forearms as he hurriedly set the grill upright and moved the lounge chairs back into place. When he was done, he rubbed his hands together and stared off toward the woods, remembering childhood days exploring around out there on his own.

Wesley did everything on his own, back then and now. In those days, it was because the other kids on the street wouldn't play with him. He was branded an untouchable weirdo early on. Even today, he was treated pretty much the same way by his supposed peers. He was twenty-three and still a virgin. In his teenaged days, his bleak prospects for ever losing his virginity had caused him a lot of inner torment. He wasn't exactly at peace with it now, but he wasn't quite so torn up about it anymore. There was more to life than just sex or lack thereof.

He was about to go back inside when he heard something move around under the deck. The fear he'd felt a few minutes ago came surging back. He cursed himself for not taking the area beneath the deck into consideration when assessing the possible danger level. The space down there was more than big enough for an average-sized person to crawl into and hide. The sound came again and this time there was nothing furtive about it.

Wesley started backing toward the door. He had his hand on the handle when the top of a blonde head popped into view. At first all he could see was the back of the person's head, but already there was something familiar about what he was seeing. He knew he should get inside and lock the door, but some instinct kept him from doing it. He strongly sensed this wasn't some ordinary intruder. A moment later, the person who'd been hiding beneath the deck emerged fully into view, getting to her feet and turning around to face him.

He gaped at the woman in disbelief.

She was Samantha Raimi, the middle-aged widow who'd lived next door for at least the last ten years. The busty blonde woman stood there in her bare feet, wearing nothing but a kimono with the sash tied tightly at her waist. Leaves and bits of dead grass were clinging to the fabric. There were more dried-up leaf fragments in her hair.

She smiled. "Hi, Wesley."

He swallowed with some difficulty and said, "Um … hi."

She started to climb the steps up to the deck. "I haven't seen you in a long time. You're looking good. Still at that community college in Monroe County?"

Wesley's hand tightened on the handle. "I don't think you

should come up here."

She laughed and said nothing in response to that. She kept climbing the steps and soon was up on the deck with him. There was maybe about eight feet of distance remaining between them. Not nearly enough to feel safe. In all the time he'd known this woman, he'd never thought of her as someone to fear. She'd always seemed so sweet and friendly. She'd also been his primary object of lust when he was a teenager. He still sometimes thought about her when he masturbated. Her physical proximity thus made him feel uptight for more reasons than one. She was still a powerfully attractive woman, but there was something undeniably off about her vibe. There was a strong hint of something predatory in it, which made no sense to Wesley.

"Why were you hiding under the deck?"

She laughed again and came another step closer. "My cat ran under there. I was trying to catch him."

"Your cat?"

Her smile widened. "Uh-huh."

Unless something had changed recently, her story didn't seem plausible. Samantha used to come over and gossip with his mother over tea in the sitting room. He'd lurk around the corner and listen to them. Their talk often turned salacious when they thought he was upstairs in his room. Listening to the hot neighbor lady talk to his mother about sex always made him feel an urgent need to jerk off. It also made him feel a little weird due to his mother's involvement. But sex wasn't all the women talked about. They chattered endlessly about lots of mundane things.

One thing he'd learned long ago was that Samantha Raimi was allergic to cats.

Samantha was another couple steps closer now.

Wesley pushed the door handle down. He felt the door come away from the frame and move incrementally inward. In another second or two, he told himself, he'd slip inside, slam the door shut, and lock it.

"That's a lie. You don't have a cat."

She chuckled and arched an eyebrow. "Oh? Is that so?"

He nodded. "You're allergic."

She waggled an admonishing finger at him. "You're a naughty boy, young Wesley. You know eavesdropping is rude."

He frowned. "Wait … you knew about that?"

"Of course. I also know you used to sneak around outside my house at night and peep in through my windows. Oh, don't look so embarrassed. I got off on letting you watch me undress. You know something, Wesley? I always sort of thought I'd be the one to deflower you. I knew you had trouble connecting with kids your age and thought maybe I could make things easier for you. Give you some confidence. I just never got around to it, unfortunately. But it's not too late. How would you like to have some fun with me?"

Wesley pushed the door open another couple inches, but continued to linger on the deck. "Did you try to get into the house?"

She laughed.

She was only a few feet away now, close enough to reach out and grab him. "Would you like to put your cock in my mouth,

Wesley? I bet you would."

She started untying the sash of her kimono.

Wesley pushed the door open another few inches and took his first tentative half-step backward. "What are you doing?"

"What does it look like I'm doing?"

She pulled open the kimono and he was able to see the bare torso beneath. He'd never been this close to a set of naked breasts and hers were massive. They were porn star breasts. The sight of them was nearly enough to short-circuit his brain and blind him to the danger the woman presented. In the next instant, however, he realized blood was smeared all over the exposed skin.

Her smile shifted, becoming more of a sneer.

"Satan wants your soul, Wesley, and I'm here to take it."

She rushed at him.

He gasped in shock and staggered backward, trying desperately to get the door shut before she could get inside. Unfortunately, he'd hesitated too long. She was already most of the way in by the time he slammed the door against her. Now she was pinned between the edge of the door and doorframe. He kept one hand on the door handle and tried to shove her back out with his other hand, but failed to budge her. His terror mounted and he screamed at her to go away. She laughed and raked her long nails across his face, drawing blood. Not just one time but multiple times, bringing forth more blood with each scrape of her nails across his vulnerable skin. And she kept laughing. His blood dripped from her fingernails to the floor.

Finally, he could take no more. He let go of the door handle and staggered back several feet, barely managing to stay upright as he came to a lurching halt and stared at his assailant through a curtain of blood. She had stopped laughing. He was no longer screaming at her. The voice of Count Gravemore was audible from the living room. He recited one of his morbid puns and did that trademark madman cackle.

Samantha came into the house and calmly closed the door. She shrugged off her kimono and stood fully naked before him. There was more blood smeared all over her body than he'd originally thought.

She looked like she'd *bathed* in it.

"Did you kill somebody?"

She nodded. "Yes."

"Why?"

"For Satan."

He grunted. "Right. Okay. How long have you been a total fucking maniac?"

She smiled. "I know you won't believe this, but I'm not crazy. Satan has ordered his followers to kill all the virgins in this town. Or at least as many as possible by midnight. And I always do as my master commands."

"How do you know I'm still a virgin?"

"I can see it. Your skin … it shimmers."

Wesley nodded slowly and wiped blood from his eyes as he started surreptitiously assessing the best potential exit routes. Her denials were meaningless. The lady definitely had a whole bucket of screws loose. He couldn't go out to the deck for the obvious reason that Samantha was in the way. There was no easy way out through the living room or the adjacent bathroom. There were windows in that direction, but they would take time to open. Too much time. That left the front door and the door to the garage. To get to the latter, he'd have to go through the kitchen and down a hall to the laundry room. The door to the garage was next to the laundry room. He could probably get there before Samantha could catch up to him, but the garage door was closed. Once inside, he'd have to turn on the light, hit the button to open it, and wait as it rolled slowly upward. Not a real option at all.

He turned and made a break for the front door.

Wesley was scared, but he thought he had a better than decent chance of getting away without absorbing further injury. She was dangerous, but she had no weapons. He was younger and faster. Escape was all but guaranteed. He dashed through an archway and into the foyer. He was almost to the front door when he felt something smash against the back of his head, driving him to his knees. Something else hit the floor with a clang. She'd grabbed something from the kitchen and thrown it at him. The heavy cast-iron coffee pot, maybe.

Before he could even attempt getting to his feet, she caught up to him and kicked him hard in the small of his back. He screeched in pain and flopped forward, his chin hitting the floor tiles hard enough to make him bite all the way through the tip of his tongue. Blood filled his mouth as he rolled onto his back and stared up at Samantha looming over him. She vaulted herself into the air above him and used her descending bare foot to piledrive his head into the floor. Wesley heard his skull fracture and knew he was doomed. She stood over him and stomped her foot down again, breaking his nose.

The foot went up and came down again.

Went up and came down again.

Samantha stomped and stomped until Wesley Campbell was dead. One of the last things he heard as consciousness slipped away was Count Gravemore's maniacal laughter once again emanating from the living room.

ELEVEN

The door to the supply closet was unlocked. This was fortunate, because the wild-eyed girl in the Cradle of Filth shirt was nearly close enough to take a lethal whack at them with her machete. A locked door would've meant certain, imminent death for one or both of them.

After getting the door open, Seth managed to drag Caitlin inside and slam it shut again just as the crazy girl was starting to swing the machete. Hearing the tip of the blade scrape against the outside of the door, he grimaced at the narrowness of the close call. If he'd been a fraction of a second slower, his blood and guts would be leaking out on the floor right now.

The sense of relief he felt was short-lived. He threw his weight against the door when it began to swing inward, making it thump emphatically back into the frame. The crazy girl screamed and started thwacking at the door with the machete. She told him to open up or he'd be sorry, advice he opted to ignore. He had a hunch he'd be a lot sorrier if he did as she said. The repeated scraping sounds from the other side of the door had his nerves jangling. He'd never been in a situation where he had to fight to stay alive. Not in real life. In video games, he'd done it thousands of times, back in the days before his parents had taken away his Xbox. This was nothing like anything he'd experienced in *Call of Duty*. He was shaking nonstop and had tears in his eyes. He'd never felt anything close to the terror he was feeling now, not even when his father was administering a disciplinary beating. He doubted his father would ever get mad enough at him to kill him. At least not on purpose.

This girl with the machete, on the other hand, absolutely *would* kill him, given even the slightest opportunity. He understood this as clearly as he'd ever understood anything. There could never be any reasoning with a person in a state of murderous frenzy. There was one other thing he also understood with great clarity. No matter how down he felt about the current state of his life, he wanted to live. To just survive and get beyond this terrible day. If he could manage that, anything might happen. His future, with all its boundless possibilities, would still be in front of him.

The girl ceased hacking at the door with the machete and started kicking it. Seth put his back against the door and got his feet braced more firmly against the floor. He reached out with his right hand, groping in the dark for the doorknob. After a few fumbling seconds, he found it and quickly determined it locked only from the outside. He'd have to keep his weight against the door in order to keep the crazy girl from getting inside the closet.

Realizing this made an already uncomfortable situation feel close to untenable. What if the crazy girl's male companion joined her in trying to kick in the door? Holding the girl back was difficult enough. The door moved a fraction of an inch inward every time she kicked it. The guy with her was bigger and probably a lot stronger. Working together, they would probably manage to force their way in eventually.

Any real chance of survival would require some help from Caitlin. He could hear her hanging back somewhere in the closet, quietly whimpering and sniffling. She seemed content to allow him to serve as her final barrier between temporary safety and certain death. Not the greatest plan ever. Thinking about how he'd acted so selflessly to save her, he felt a twitch of resentment.

It was time for her to step up.

"Caitlin?"

He raised his voice.

"Caitlin!"

She let out a frightened little squeak and replied in a small voice. "What?"

The crazy girl stopped kicking the door and threw her weight against it. Seth had to stiffen his back and redouble the physical effort necessary to keep her out. "If you want to live, you're gonna need to help me. Try to find the light switch in here."

Caitlin sniffled. "Okay."

He heard her start to come toward him as the crazy girl threw her weight against the door again. She was moving with the expected tentativeness of someone moving around in an unfamiliar room in the dark. At one point she bumped into some shelving and caused some cleaning products to fall off a shelf and land with a clatter on the floor. She yelped in surprise but kept feeling her way toward him. He held his breath as he sensed her getting to within a few feet of him. Despite the dire situation, this was still his dream girl, the one he fantasized about while lying in bed at night. So now he felt nervous in addition to terrified. He heard her hand slap against the wall to his left as she started feeling around for the light switch.

Not finding it there, she brushed against him as she sought to continue her search along the section of wall to his right. For a fleeting moment, her breasts were pressed against his chest. He could feel her breath on his face. An inappropriate urge to lean in for a kiss came and went as the crazy girl flung herself against the other side of the door yet again. She was screeching at them and her frenzied state was only intensifying. Most of what she was saying was rendered incoherent by the shrillness of those screeches, but every once in a while Seth could make out a word or two.

The one repeated most often was "Caitlin".

"Do you know that crazy bitch?"

The closet abruptly filled with bright light, forcing Seth to squint for a moment. Then he turned his head to the right and saw Caitlin staring at him with a grim expression.

"She's my sister. We're … estranged."

The surprise he felt at this revelation was enough to render him temporarily incapable of response. He remembered his initial impression of something subtly familiar in the crazy girl's features. At first he figured he'd simply seen her somewhere before, but now he realized that impression of familiarity was actually some part of his mind perceiving the family resemblance between Caitlin and her crazy sister.

Seth's belated response was, "Wow."

Caitlin grunted. "Yeah. Hard to believe, right?"

"You can say that again. Holy shit."

Some moments elapsed before Seth realized Caitlin's sister had stopped trying to force her way into the closet. He had no doubt this was only a temporary respite. She would start up again soon, probably with the help of her accomplice. Eventually they would get in and that would be the end of Seth and Caitlin. Unless, of course, they could successfully fortify the door and hold out in here until the police arrived. He was about to say something to this effect when a voice spoke from the other side of the door.

"Caitlin? Can you hear me?"

It was the crazy girl again, but she sounded calmer now, speaking in a normal tone rather than screeching at them. Other sounds could now be heard drifting in from the basement. Moaning and sobbing. Pitiful pleas for mercy. And something else. A wet, meaty sound, one that made Seth think of a butcher cutting into a side of beef with a cleaver. His stomach fluttered queasily when he realized what he was hearing. The crazy girl's companion was hacking away at the dwindling number of surviving youth group members. He heard people scream and then fall silent as the machete sliced down yet again.

Caitlin wiped tears from her face and sniffled again. "I hear you."

The crazy girl laughed in a softly insidious way. "There's no way you're getting out of here. You know that, right? There's no one left to save you or raise the alarm. You're trapped. But if you let me in, I promise I'll make it quick. You won't suffer."

"Why are you doing this?"

"Let me in and I'll tell you."

Caitlin grunted. "I don't think so."

"Let me in, you sanctimonious little bitch," the crazy girl said, her tone rising sharply again. She thumped the base of a fist against the door, making Seth flinch after the all-too-brief lull. "Let me in so I can see what you look like on the fucking inside."

She laughed and thumped her fist against the door again.

The closet's interior was roughly the size of a standard bathroom in an average suburban home. Maybe just a shade bigger than that. There were two sets of metal shelves against the back wall and another set against the wall to Seth's left. Along with the expected cleaning supplies, stacks of bibles, prayer manuals, and other religious instruction texts lined the gunmetal gray shelves. Caitlin had been cowering in that corner to the left before coming forward at Seth's request. The shelving unit to the left was the one she'd bumped against. That this bit of incidental content had been enough to send bottles of Windex and Clorox tumbling to the floor suggested the shelving units weren't bracketed to the walls.

The crazy girl kicked the door.

Seth grimaced and locked eyes with Caitlin. "You're gonna have to do something for me. Come here a minute."

After a brief hesitation, she did as he asked, approaching him as her lunatic sister displayed signs of building toward a frenzy again, kicking the door and occasionally hacking at it with the machete. He beckoned her even closer and she obliged. Her eyes widened when he put his mouth to her ear and whispered his plan to her.

She pulled back a step and stared at him with a dubious expression. Then her gaze flicked over to the shelving units against the back wall and back to him. "Those look heavy. I don't think I can do it."

Seth shook his head. "But you can. All you have to do is give that one right there a good, hard shove. Gravity will do the rest."

In eyeballing the distance between the door and the back wall, Seth estimated the top part of the shelving unit would fall against the door at roughly waist-level, forming an effective wedge against anyone trying to force their way inside. He had a high level of confidence that this would work. The complicating factor was time. The crazy girl's lanky male accomplice would surely soon join her in attempting to knock the door open. He knew he wouldn't be able to withstand their combined effort.

Seth mouthed the word "please".

Caitlin shrugged. "I'll try."

She went over to the back wall and reached a hand behind the indicated shelving unit. Before doing as he'd asked, she looked at him again, doubt still etched in her pretty features. "You won't be able to get out of the way in time."

He smiled. "Sure I will. I'll duck down at the last fucking second. Just go ahead and do it, okay?"

She nodded, her expression somber but determined now. "Okay."

She gave the shelving unit a shove and it started to topple forward. Books and magazines fell to the concrete floor in piles. Right as Seth was about to hit the deck, the crazy girl jabbed the machete in under the door. The tip of the blade punched through the back of his shoe and sliced into the heel of his right foot.

Seth screamed and fell forward.

TWELVE

Micah stood in the center of the basement with the blood-caked machete hanging limp in his hand. He turned in a slow circle, struck almost numb with horror by the sheer scope of what he'd done. There was nowhere he could look without seeing gaudy, bright red splashes of blood or dismembered body pieces.

They were all dead now, except for the two hiding in the closet. Two bodies in these latest additions to their ledger of the dead belonged to Sindie, but the rest were all his. One, two, three, four, five of them. Five lives he'd snuffed out in a blind panic. With Sindie fixated on the two in the closet, it'd been left to him to exercise a brutal and bloody form of crowd control.

In his entire life, he'd never actively wanted to kill anyone, yet here he was with all this blood on his hands. He'd done it because he didn't want any of the youth group members getting away and running off to summon the cops while he and Sindie were still here. Not out of concern for himself, but for Sindie. These were murders committed in the name of love. He didn't want her winding up in jail. A girl like her didn't belong there, regardless of anything she'd done. She was too pretty. Too smart. Too talented. She was meant for bigger things. Fame and adulation. He acted in the interest of saving her future.

His sense of panic spiraled out of control as he herded the teenagers around the room, dashing here and there at breakneck speed to keep them from getting to the door, swinging the machete whenever any of them miscalculated and got within range. Sometimes he slipped in the ever-widening pools of blood and crashed to the floor, but so did they. He kept scrambling back to his feet and chasing them down, hacking away with wild abandon until just one was left. The one who almost got away, a slender auburn-haired beauty who managed to get around him and break for the door while he was busy trying to wrench his machete out of a dead guy's skull. She made it to the door and got halfway up the staircase before he caught up to her and rammed the machete into her back. This was done with enough force that the blade went all the way through her body and emerged through her abdomen. He held the girl in his arms in her dying seconds, crying and whispering apologies.

Then he carried the body back down to the basement and set it gingerly on the floor. Sindie didn't so much as glance his way.

She only cared about the kids in the closet. For now, there was room for nothing else in her world. Her inattention left him in an emotional vacuum, allowing depression to seep in along with a heavy dose of unwelcome introspection.

This horrendous thing he'd done ... it wasn't who he really was. The furthest thing from it. He was a good guy, a guy who'd never meant anyone any harm. Except none of that was true anymore and never would be again. There was no taking any of this back. His soul was tainted forever. He flashed back to his brief flirtations with the notion of escape and wished like hell he'd acted on the impulse.

He stopped turning in a circle and stared at Sindie. The machete slipped from his fingers and clattered on the floor. She still didn't glance his way. She'd resumed yelling at the kids in the closet and pounding on the door.

Without really thinking about what he was doing, he turned away from her and eyed the open door in the far corner of the room. He'd neglected to kick the door shut again when carrying the auburn-haired girl's body back into the basement. From here he was able to glimpse the bottom few stairs through the open doorway. In another moment, he started walking in that direction. He waited to hear Sindie call out to him, but she never did. If she had, he would've stayed. He reached the staircase and started climbing. Halfway up, he paused, giving Sindie one last chance to call him back down.

She didn't.

He kept going.

Before long, he was back outside in the sunlight. It was late afternoon getting toward early evening. That fall chill was in the air again. Sirens were blaring somewhere in the distance. A lot of them, from the sound of it. He wasn't worried about that. They weren't coming this way. This was a town awash in chaos and confusion. Littleburg's legion of Satanists were out in force, collecting pure souls wherever they could be found. Feeling no need for hurry, Micah took his time ambling across the parking lot toward Sindie's Kia Sorento. The spare key Sindie had given him after buying the SUV a month ago was in his pocket. He took it out as he reached the vehicle and hit the unlock button on the key fob.

Micah didn't feel bad about taking Sindie's car for the simple reason of having no other options. He was moving through the world now in a steadily thickening haze and willfully not thinking about much of anything. The numbness that had overcome him in the aftermath of the basement massacre felt like it might become a permanent thing. He couldn't imagine a life spent feeling this way.

He couldn't imagine a life.

The route he took out of town allowed him to see ample evidence of the Luciferic darkness overtaking the community. There were bodies in the street, gunned down, run down, or hacked to pieces with various edged weapons. Others dangled from tree limbs and power lines. One was nailed to an upside down cross in front of a church. Cops and other first responders were out answering calls, but it looked to Micah as if they were merely going through the motion, doing the bare minimum for show. Later on, this would give them a level of plausible deniability should any concerned citizens of Littleburg attempt to alert outside authorities as to what had happened here. It all corresponded very neatly with what Sindie had told him at the beginning of this madness. The Satanists were in control here. They ran things and were in charge of the official narrative. What was happening here today looked like the apocalypse, but soon enough there would be little discernible trace of it. Much of the carnage he was seeing blended in seamlessly with the ubiquitous Halloween decorations anyway.

He was on a narrow and winding stretch of State Road 96 on the outskirts of town when he saw the woman step out of the woods and into the middle of the road. She stopped there and turned toward him. The numbness enveloping him in the aftermath of what he'd done at the church was pierced by a new sense of wariness. A tingle went up his spine as he drew near the woman and realized who she was.

The priestess.

She was wearing the heavy velvet cape he'd seen her wear at each of the midnight masses he'd attended. That white plague mask with the long beak again covered the top half of her face. Beneath the cape, she was nude. Her chin jutted defiantly outward, as if daring him to run her over.

He tried to picture himself doing it. The interstate junction was about a half mile beyond where she stood. Despite the hopeless feelings gripping him, he was aware a part of his subconscious mind had been leading him in this direction all along. This was his exit from madness. His portal to freedom. And this strange woman stood in the way of it. He sat in the Sorento with his foot on the brake a while longer, fretting about what to do. Now that he was this close to being gone from this rotten place, he felt the tantalizing allure of something other than oblivion. This horror he'd experienced could be put behind him. He could work on forgetting what he'd done. Life could be okay again somewhere else.

Somewhere far away.

Then he heard her voice in his head.

Come to me.

After putting the SUV in park, Micah got out and began to walk toward her, leaving the door open and the engine running. He did this with no thought of hastily retreating to the SUV and driving away. There was no contingency plan here. He did it because it was the easiest thing to do. He wouldn't be needing those keys again and he didn't care if someone came along and stole the Sorento. The only reason he bothered putting the SUV in park was because exiting a vehicle that was standing still was easier than getting out of one that was still moving. There were things he did instinctually, without conscious thought. There was no room in his head now for anything other than the priestess and doing as she commanded.

Below the surface, a faint and distant part of him was worried. He didn't seem to be in control of his own body. An outside consciousness had invaded his mind and was somehow compelling him to do what it wanted. A consciousness that might not have his best interests in mind. The woman standing in the road was no ordinary human female. She might not be human at all. She might instead be some kind of creature beyond his understanding. A succubus or some other kind of demon. A supernatural entity, the existence of which would terrify any sane person in control of their own faculties. That description, however, was one that no longer fit Micah.

He got to within a few feet of her and dropped to his knees in submission. It seemed like the right thing to do. He'd tried to get away, which was obviously not allowed. He was showing his acquiescence, his surrender to her will.

"Stand."

This time she spoke with her own voice rather than transmitting a message to his brain. The effect was the same. Her voice conveyed an authority that was absolute. Disobedience was not possible.

He got to his feet and bowed his head. "I'm sorry I tried to leave. I know it was wrong."

She reached out to touch his face with her fingers. He shuddered at the physical contact, becoming instantly erect. Her touch vibrated with some of the magic he'd felt in the woods last night.

"You can never leave this place," she told him, stroking his skin with her fingertips. "You belong here. You belong to Satan."

He nodded. "I know. It won't happen again."

Her hand came away from his face and her fingertips glided lightly down his chest and came to a stop at his abdomen. "You're right about that."

She tore away his shirt and punched her splayed fingers into his lower abdomen. Elongated fingernails that were now more like talons parted his flesh and began to dig around in his guts. Mind-bending agony ripped through him, but he was unable to scream or attempt to get away. Her iron will kept him in place as she tore out his intestines and wrapped them around his throat. More organs and a lot of blood spilled out of the open abdominal cavity, landing with a series of wet, squishy plops on the faded and pitted backwoods asphalt.

Micah didn't die right away.

The priestess exerted her will again, keeping him upright and cognizant for several more minutes. She did this so he could have a prolonged pain experience. And because she derived immense pleasure from his suffering.

After she finally let him die, she dragged his corpse into the woods. He would make a fine meal later that night.

THIRTEEN

The real name of the man known to generations of Channel 39 viewers as Count Victor von Gravemore was Morrie Goldman. Morrie had a genuine affinity for horror films that dated back to his childhood in the 1950s. His favorites were still the ones that first sparked his love of the genre. The Universal monster films and countless b-movies he saw at Saturday matinees as a child. They captured his imagination and inspired him in ways that resonated deeply with him to this day. Throughout his career as a horror host, he'd been hearing from viewers about how his show was what got them through some of the toughest times in their lives. Hearing this always warmed his heart, and when he thought about it in private moments, knowing he'd touched so many lives in a positive way brought a tear to his eyes.

What his viewers didn't know was the same was true for him. The show was what he lived for, the thing that kept him going through all these lonely decades. He was fortunate the show had endured for so long and against all odds. When it first started, he'd been given a ten-week tryout contract. This came after months of relentlessly lobbying the station manager with his pitch for the show. The manager was skeptical. He said horror host shows were "old hat", besides which he had a hard time believing horror-centric programming could succeed in such a conservative community. To the man's great surprise, the ratings were strong from the start and actually improved in subsequent weeks.

Morrie was given a substantial pay hike and a longer contract, which the station had routinely renewed every year since then. In those early years, he hadn't imagined he would still be at it several decades later. When he was young, he'd harbored dreams of moving to Hollywood and getting into the movie business as a performer. He yearned to see himself on the screen alongside his heroes. The ones who were still alive by the time he became a young man, anyway. People like Vincent Price and Christopher Lee.

Alas, this aspiration was never realized. Doing a show in a small town was one thing. The audience wasn't big and thus the pressure of performing adequately wasn't more than he could handle. Unfortunately, he lacked the confidence needed to uproot his life and move all the way across the country to a huge, bustling city he was sure would feel like an alien world. It scared him in a big way and eventually he let go of that dream.

He still felt some wistfulness whenever he thought about his years of trying to talk himself into taking that risk. The intervening decades had taken much of the edge off his regret, however, and consequently he didn't think about those days very often. Things could have turned out much worse for Morrie Goldman. He'd made a comfortable life for himself doing something he loved and had made a career out of celebrating his favorite film genre.

After all these years, *Shock Theater* remained Channel 39's most popular piece of locally produced programming. Thus he was not overly worried when he was summoned to the station manager's office at the end of the final host segment for *Motel Hell.* His only concern at that point was the time factor. Getting from his set to Greg MacReady's office would take several minutes, then of course he'd need several more minutes to get back to the set after the meeting concluded. Without even factoring in the length of the meeting, he'd be cutting it close to get back in time to do the intro segment for *Videodrome.*

His initial impulse was to decline the invitation. No meeting with the station manager could possibly be short enough to allow for a timely return to set. "Perhaps Mr. MacReady has forgotten," he told the young intern who'd been sent to fetch him. "Today is Halloween and I am in the midst of hosting an all-day horror marathon, just as I have every year for decades. I'm not sure how an event of this magnitude could possibly slip his mind, but it must be so because otherwise he would surely know I will not have an opportunity to visit his office until after the marathon is over. Explain this to Mr. MacReady and pass along my apologies."

The gangly intern was thin to the point of looking starved. His protruding Adam's apple was among the most prominent Goldman had ever seen. There was something almost grotesque about it. It was especially noticeable when the young man was nervous.

Like now.

"I just can't do that, Mr. Goldman. Mr. MacReady told me not to take no for an answer." The intern's face was red and he was speaking in a higher register than usual, a reedy tone that grated on Goldman's ears. "He knows the marathon is still going and he said to tell you it doesn't matter. Attendance is mandatory, not optional. Um, his words, not mine. Obviously. I'm sorry, Mr. Goldman, but you really need to go."

Goldman frowned. "Jesus. What's so all-fired important that he has to see me *right now?*"

The intern shrugged. "I don't know, Mr. Goldman. He wouldn't say. I'm sorry."

About eight minutes later he was standing outside the closed door to MacReady's office. He was still more irritated than concerned, but by then a tiny dollop of worry had entered his mind. There had been little room in his head today for anything other than the marathon, always the most important day of the year for his show, but between segments he'd heard a bit about the strange wave of violence taking place throughout Littleburg. According to his crew, reports of violent acts were continuing to come in with no indication yet of the strange outbreak beginning to ebb. He didn't believe Channel 39 would cut the marathon short to go to breaking news coverage of the developing story, but something like that could explain why he'd been ordered to MacReady's office.

He knocked on the door and opened it when he heard the manager say, "Come in."

The office was small and unassuming, the opposite of what an outsider might expect for the boss of a television station. It looked more like the office of a junior accountant at a small firm, with the inexpensive, second-rate furnishings and the piles of haphazardly stacked paperwork on MacReady's desk. An executive at a station in an even moderately larger market would definitely have a more impressive desk than the embarrassing office supply store reject MacReady sat behind. Channel 39, however, wasn't even really a small market station. Littleburg was more of a micro-market. Its operating budget was a reflection of this reality. Nobody was getting rich at Channel 39, not even the man behind revered local institution Count Victor von Gravemore.

MacReady rose from his seat behind the desk and the two men shook hands, with the manager then gesturing for Goldman to sit in the chair opposite the desk. Goldman did so as MacReady sat down again.

Goldman frowned as he glanced to his right. Three people he recognized were crowded into the little couch against the side wall there. One was a middle-aged man named Hal Meyer. Hal was Channel 39's programming director. At the opposite end of the couch was Jerry Russell, a studio technician. Seated between these men was the channel's evening news anchor, Joyce Mitchell. Other than Goldman himself, the bottle-blonde stunner was the closest thing the station had to a star. All three had rubber masks clutched tightly in their laps.

Goldman looked at MacReady. "What's going on here?" Another rubber mask was face-down on the station manager's desk, with only its white interior visible. "Did you call me in here to tell me you're all going to a Halloween party and are leaving me in charge? Because I'm afraid I'm not up to the task, not with the marathon still going on."

MacReady chuckled. "That's not why I called you in here, Morrie." He rearranged his features in a way meant to convey a shift to a more somber demeanor, but he didn't quite succeed. The expression looked forced. He was unable to conceal the trace of a smirk at one corner of his mouth. "I'm afraid I have some bad news. There's no easy way to say this, so I'll just say it." He heaved an exaggerated sigh. "Morrie … we've decided to let you go. It's time to take the station in a new direction."

Goldman gasped and felt a tightness in his chest. "This has to be a joke. How can you cancel *Shock Theater*? My ratings are still good."

"Who said anything about canceling the show? We're not doing that, Morrie." MacReady grabbed the rubber mask from his desk and rose from his chair. He came around to the front of the desk and stared down at Goldman. "You're old, Morrie. Really, really old."

Joyce Mitchell tittered at these remarks. "No shit. He's got more wrinkles than a fucking mummy."

The men seated to either side of her laughed.

MacReady nodded, smiling now. "You see, Morrie, we've decided we need to appeal to a new generation. *Shock Theater* will carry on without you, but with a new host. We'll be reaching out to a popular local artist next week to see if she's interested in taking the reins from you. Maybe you've heard of her? Her name's Sindie Midnight. Very hot lady."

Joyce Mitchell made an appreciative noise. "Mmm. You can say that again. She's sexy as hell. I sat on her face at the mass last night. It was the absolute *best.*"

Goldman's look of deep confusion grew even more pronounced. "The last what? What the hell are you people talking about? You can't get a new host. There is no show without me. I *am Shock Theater.*"

The three on the couch stood and took up positions behind Goldman, who turned in his seat to glare at them for a moment before again focusing on MacReady. "You can't just suddenly fire me with no good justification. I have a contract. This is an outrage. You'll be hearing from my lawyer if you go through with this. As for this bullshit meeting, I'm done with it."

He got to his feet and wheeled about with the intent of storming out of the room. The other three were blocking the way. He might have attempted to bull his way through them, but they had donned their masks and he was quite taken aback by what he now saw. Each mask replicated the famous countenance of a different horror icon from the past. Hal wore the face of Boris Karloff as Frankenstein's Monster. Joyce Mitchell was wearing a Vampira mask. Jerry had picked out a Vincent Price mask for the occasion. The masks alone were strange enough, but each of them was also wielding a knife. Knives that, until now, had been hidden in their laps under the masks.

Goldman was starting to feel real fear when he turned around again and projected his outrage at MacReady, who had yet to put on his mask. "You should all be ashamed of yourselves. I've been at this station longer than most of you have been alive. I deserve respect. I don't deserve to be the victim of some childish prank."

MacReady smirked. "This isn't a prank. "We're going to kill you now, Morrie. There's just something I have to know first. How the hell did you get to seventy-fucking-three-years-old without ever once fucking anybody? I just don't get how that's even possible."

Joyce Mitchell laughed. "God, just look at him. It's no mystery. He's hideous. Motherfucker makes the monsters in all those *Shock Theater* movies look like beauty queens."

Goldman had no response for the woman's insult. He was still too stunned by what he'd heard MacReady say. It was true he'd gone his entire life without ever once being sexually intimate with another human being, but he'd never discussed that fact with anyone. Never even vaguely alluded to it. Not once.

He shook his head slowly in abject disbelief. "How could you possibly know that?"

Instead of immediately answering, MacReady finally pulled on his mask. A rubber facsimile of Christopher Lee was now staring back at Goldman. MacReady also held a knife now. "Your wrinkly old skin has that virgin shimmer. It's a Satanic cult thing. You wouldn't understand. Anywho, I can see you're confused about the masks. These are actually a final tribute to you for all your years of loyal service to Channel 39. Feel free to pretend you're dying at the hands of your old-time horror heroes. Before we get to that, though ... come on, be real. Tell us how you made it through almost three quarters of a fucking century without once getting laid."

Goldman sighed. "I'm just not interested in sex. Never have been."

Joyce Mitchell said, "What a weirdo."

The men all laughed.

Channel 39's station manager stepped forward and rammed his knife into Goldman's stomach. The pain was horrendous. Morrie Goldman had never experienced anything like it. He wanted to scream or cry out for help, but he didn't have the strength. The other three converged on him then, burying their knives deep in his flesh in different locations. They pulled the blades out and quickly jabbed them in again several more times in rapid succession.

After being stabbed close to two dozen times, Morrie Goldman fell to the floor and stared up at them. He saw the faces of the horror elite peering down at him, blood dripping in steady patters to the floor from the knives they held.

He smiled as his vision began to fade.

FOURTEEN

Seth missed getting his head smashed in by the shelving unit as it toppled forward by a tiny fraction of an inch. He heard Caitlin scream as he landed hard on the concrete floor. The top of his head was right up against the bottom of the shelving unit. He needed to scoot backwards slightly in order to get out from under it, but the pain from his sliced-up heel made accomplishing that easier said than done. Before he could even try, Caitlin's crazy sister jabbed the machete under the door again. This time the tip of the blade punched through the bottom of the shoe it'd already perforated once before. About an inch of steel stabbed him through the underside of his foot.

He screamed and heard the crazy girl laugh as she jabbed the machete under the door yet again. This time he managed to jerk his foot out of the way in time to avoid absorbing yet another puncture wound, but this was only a temporary reprieve. He needed to push through the pain and maneuver himself away from the door. Trying to twist around required flexing his injured foot, which intensified the pain significantly. Tears filled his eyes and for a moment he began to think it was hopeless. The machete jabbed in under the door again and this time the blade cut through his jeans and sliced a bloody line along his shin. He screamed. Then Caitlin had her hands on him and was dragging him away from the door. She was stronger than he ever would have guessed. Maybe it was adrenaline. Or maybe she worked out a lot. Whatever the case, he was grateful.

She dragged him over to the corner where she'd been cowering earlier. It was well out of the way of any weapon the crazy girl could slide under the door. Aside from maybe a gun, but she didn't have one. Not that he'd seen anyway. That didn't mean she couldn't go out and get one from somewhere, but he didn't think she would. This was an insane thing that was happening here, but there had to be a limit to how long it could continue. At some point someone would find out what was going on and call the cops. It would come to an end one way or another, probably sooner than later. All they had to do now was outwait the crazy girl and her lanky boyfriend.

Caitlin pulled a trembling Seth into her arms and whispered calming things into his ears. Despite his pain, it slowly began to work. Being held and comforted by his dream girl was such a weird thing. Feeling her body crushed against his was so nice. It was too bad so many innocent people had to die for this to happen, but he was enjoying the feeling anyway. He wondered if this made him a bad person. He thought it probably did. A little bit anyway.

After realizing he was no longer in range of the machete, the crazy girl went back to kicking the door and screaming at them to come out. With the heavy shelving unit braced against it now, however, the door didn't move inward or rattle as much in its frame with each kick. Seth was pretty sure she would have no chance of smashing her way in now.

His trembling had nearly ceased by the time he said, "Why are they doing this? Are they crazy?"

Caitlin made a contemplative sound. "My sister's always been a little … off. She used to have horrible, screaming fights with my parents. She threatened to kill us all a bunch of times. When she left us and moved in with some guy at sixteen, my parents could've gotten the law involved and forced her to come back, but they didn't bother. We finally had a peaceful house again. It was a relief. So, yeah, I guess maybe she's crazy, but I never seriously believed she'd kill anybody until today."

Seth frowned. "I wonder what finally made her snap."

"It's not just them, Seth."

He pulled partly out of her embrace and turned his head to look her in the eye. "What do you mean?"

"The whole town's going crazy. A bunch of us were getting texts about it before we lost service. Something started jamming the signal, probably to stop word from getting out. There's a lot of random violence happening. Murders. Dozens of them, I think. Maybe more."

Seth's expression conveyed disbelief. "That's insane. Why would something like this be happening in Littleburg?"

Caitlin hesitated a moment before responding, a crease forming in the center of her forehead as she appeared to weigh the veracity of what she was about to say. "First off, this is crazy. I know that. But there's a rumor going around, something passed on by people who survived attacks, I guess. They're saying the killers are specifically targeting ... well, virgins."

"Huh?"

"People who've never had sex."

Seth grunted. "I know what a virgin is. I just don't get it. Why do that?"

"Because Satan commanded it. To collect pure souls."

Seth laughed. "Satan? Come on."

Caitlin's expression was intensely serious. "I'm not joking, Seth. I can show you the texts I was getting if you want. It's all in there. All the attackers are saying they're doing this for Satan. My sister said it, too. Don't you remember the crazy shit they were yelling when they came into the basement?"

After reflecting back a moment, it did come back to him. "Oh, yeah. You're right. At the time I thought it was just them making a weird joke. For, like, a Halloween prank. In my defense, it was right before they actually started killing everybody. Wait ... how do they know who's a virgin and who isn't?"

Caitlin sighed. "I don't know. They just look at you and ...

see it. Somehow."

"That makes no goddamned sense."

A chuckle came from the other side of the door. "She's right, you know. My baby sister has always been a smart little bitch. A sickening goody two-shoes, but smart. Satan gave us the power to see your fucking virgin sparkle."

Somehow Seth hadn't realized Caitlin's crazy sister had stopped trying to break down the door until she spoke.

Caitlin raised her voice and said, "Could you please just go away, Cynthia? You can't get in here. There must be loads of other virgins you could kill somewhere else."

More laughter from the deranged sister. "No can do, sis. I love my dark master, but I love myself even more. I have to kill you before I can get back to doing the devil's work. I need this. I need to see the look on your face as I cut your throat."

Still more demented laughter.

Then there was a prolonged lapse in the conversation. Caitlin and Seth said nothing as they held each other and listened to the crazy girl hum a tune neither recognized. Strangely, it had an almost hymn-like quality.

After several minutes of this, Seth reflexively jumped when he felt Caitlin's hand on his crotch. She squeezed him through his jeans and kissed the side of his head. He gave her a confused look. "What are you doing?"

She kissed him again, this time on the mouth. "I'm doing what I have to do. What *we* have to do. What other kids like us are doing all over town to save themselves." She squeezed his crotch again and pulled at his zipper tab as she gave him another kiss on the mouth. "Take your penis out, Seth."

She was speaking in the softest of whispers. He dropped his voice to the same level for his reply. "Are you sure about this?"

She nodded and moaned almost inaudibly. "I am. I always believed in preserving my virginity until my wedding night, but if we don't do this, I may never have a wedding night. We have to remove the thing that makes us targets. After we do this, we'll be safe. And God will understand why we had to do it. Come on, take it out." Another of those nearly inaudible moans. "I want to see it. I really do."

Seth couldn't believe his ears. He'd spent so much time fantasizing about this gorgeous girl, all while being completely certain he could never actually get with her. Until now she had never looked twice at him. More than once at YALL meetings he'd noticed her purposely avoiding eye contact with him. Aloof and snooty. That had always been his impression of Caitlin. It wasn't just a matter of perception. She had always associated only with other popular, good-looking kids. There was no doubt she deliberately excluded people she deemed lesser from her social circle, including him.

And now she wanted to fuck him. Yes, it was to save her own skin, but that didn't change the essential fact. His unattainable dream girl wanted to fuck him. The world had officially turned upside-down. Strangely, her sexual excitement seemed genuine. All those soft little moans were inflaming his own arousal. She kept kissing him and telling him to take it out.

So he did.

She started breathing harder when she saw his erect cock. Then she gripped it and he almost came right away. Sensing this, she ripped her hand away and jumped to her feet. She wiggled quickly out of her panties, lifted her skirt, and lowered herself to him. He gasped loudly when he felt her guide him into her.

It didn't last long. Less than a minute, actually. But what did it matter? They both started laughing when it was over. Relief swept over them. They were no longer virgins. The danger was over, at least in terms of being targets for random marauding Satanists. The crazy sister was another story, though. This was a personal grudge. She might have a hard time letting go of it.

Laughter again came from the other side of the door, but it was more subdued than before, with perhaps a note of defeat in it. "Congrats, sis. Yeah, I heard what you were doing in there. Nice attempt at trying to keep it quiet, though. Gotta say, I didn't see this coming. I was sure you'd keep your chastity vow intact no matter what, even if it meant taking it to the grave with you. God's probably all pissed off at you now."

She laughed again.

Caitlin climbed off of Seth and turned about to glare at the door. "Can you please just go away now? We're no longer of any use to you as far as your master is concerned. If you're still determined to kill me, just know I'm willing to stay in here all night if necessary. You won't get nearly as many virgin kills as your crazy friends. I think God might forgive my moment of weakness under the circumstances. Can you say the same of your master?"

Silence from the other side of the door.

Caitlin grunted. "Didn't think so. I kind of feel like the devil is a little less forgiving in general than my lord and savior. Do you really want to let him down?"

Another lengthy silence ensued as the question hung in the air. At last, a heavy sigh came from the other side of the door. "Okay, sis. You win. For now. But don't think for a minute this is over. I'll circle back around to you eventually and finish this. See you later, bitch."

Another moment later, they heard footsteps walking away from the door. They grew steadily fainter and then they heard the slam of a door. Caitlin scooted away from the corner and crawled under the fallen shelving unit. Seth tensed as she put her face to the floor and peeked out through the narrow gap under the door. It was too easy to picture that machete suddenly jabbing in through that gap and puncturing Caitlin's eye. He remained tense as she stayed in that vulnerable position an uncomfortable while longer.

Finally, she crawled back out from under the shelving unit and got to her feet. She approached Seth and held out a hand. "Come on. Get up."

Only then did he realize his wilting penis was still partly exposed. Embarrassed, he tucked it away, zipped up, and buttoned his pants. Then he took Caitlin's hand and allowed her to haul him to his feet. The pain from his injured foot came back with a vengeance when he unthinkingly applied pressure to it. He yelped and lifted the heel off the floor. Grimacing, he realized getting around for the next little bit would require a lot of awkward hopping. Oh, well. Being temporarily hobbled beat the hell out of being killed. He was lucky. A doctor would fix him up soon and before long he'd be back to more or less normal.

Working together, they managed to get the shelving unit raised upright and out of the way again. When that was done, Caitlin went to the door and eased it open a tiny crack. Seth tensed again, still expecting a sudden thrust of the machete through the gap, but that didn't happen. He was being paranoid, of course. They'd both heard her leave and slam the basement door behind her.

Caitlin glanced over her shoulder at Seth. "Coast looks clear. You ready to go?"

He nodded nervously. "Yeah. I think so."

"Good. Just a warning, though. It looks like a slaughterhouse out here."

Seth let out a shuddery breath and nodded again. "I can deal with it. All I really care about is getting the fuck out of here."

She smiled. "Me, too."

Seth was right behind her as she pulled the door open and began to step out of the closet. His first glimpse of the basement was from an angle over her right shoulder. It was more than enough to confirm her grim assessment of the landscape. The sheer amount of blood spattered all over seemingly everything was staggering and disturbing. He was on the verge of emerging from the closet when his gaze went to the closed basement door in the far corner of the room and he spied the pair of black Doc Martens on the floor there.

"Hi, sis."

Caitlin gasped and turned toward the sound of her sister's voice. In that same instant, a machete swung down and chopped hard into the top of her head. Seth gaped at this grisly sight in horrified surprise as Caitlin's sister came away from her position against the wall and wrenched the machete free. She swung it again before her sister's body could topple to the floor. This time the blade ripped open her throat. She was dead by the time she hit the floor.

Even in the midst of shock, Seth understood what had happened. The crazy sister had walked away, traversing the blood-soaked floor all the way to the door. After slamming the door to feign her exit, she removed her shoes and crept back across the floor in her bare feet. Then she put her back against the wall next to the closet door and waited for them to come out. Seth cursed their shortsightedness and impatience. If only they'd waited a while longer, the sister Caitlin had called Cynthia might really have given up and gone away.

Cynthia was positively beaming as she turned away from her dead sister and faced Seth. She looked like she'd just won the lottery. "You have no idea how satisfying that was. I'm sure that bitch fed you a line of shit about me while you two were locked up in there, but I'm here to tell you there's two sides to every story. My family hated me because they couldn't tolerate anything that didn't conform to their repressed way of thinking. I was in hell for years before I found Satan."

Seth nodded warily as he absorbed this speech. He wasn't sure why she was bothering to mount any kind of justification for what she'd done. With his wounded heel, he was no kind of threat to her. Any attempt at escape would be laughable.

"So what now? You kill me?"

She shrugged. "I could do that, sure. I might even enjoy it, even though you're no longer a virgin. Or I could bring you to tonight's midnight mass and see if the priestess thinks you're worthy of becoming one of us. What do you say, boy? I get this vibe from you, sort of a kindred feeling. You know what it's like to be scorned and treated like shit, don't you?"

Seth frowned, thinking about his parents.

He thought about his father's fists connecting with his face. He had to admit Caitlin's sister had a point.

"So what are you saying? That I become a Satanist like you?"

She smiled. "That's exactly what I'm saying, kid. And, hey, it looks like I need a new escort to tonight's big bash, as my boyfriend seems to have run away. I loved the guy, but I can't say I'm surprised. He was always so wishy-washy about the devil worship thing. Another thing to consider. We're actively working to convert the whole town to the dark faith. Things won't go well for those who can't get on board with that."

Seth sighed. "What the hell. Why not? I'll go to this midnight mass thing with you."

In part he said this because it was the pragmatic thing to do.

He feared a negative answer might cause him to fall victim to that machete, leaving him dead on the floor like all the others who'd come to the midweek YALL meeting. On another level, he was genuinely intrigued by Cynthia's invitation.

"You've made a wise decision, kid. What's your name, by the way?"

"Seth."

"Well, Seth, judging from the way you're holding your foot up like that, you could probably use some help getting out of here."

She extended her free hand and he took it after a brief hesitation. As they started moving toward the basement door, she squeezed his hand hard and said, "Careful about all the blood. It's slippery as hell."

The bonfire at that night's midnight mass was the biggest ever, with the bodies of those killed throughout the day feeding the flames. Micah's body was among those that burned that night. Sindie glimpsed his face in the huge pile of bodies moments before the pile was set ablaze. She felt sad when she saw his slack features and realized he was gone forever. Her love for him had been real, their emotional connection deeper and more profound than nearly anything else she'd ever known, with the obvious exception of her love for Satan.

The dark lord made another appearance at the mass, again inhabiting the body of the masked priestess to deliver his message. He was pleased with the unprecedented bounty of pure souls delivered to him by his faithful that night. The souls taken in his name would feed his power and help to bring about a new dark age. The reward for those who served him would be just as unprecedented. Soon Littleburg's followers of the dark faith would hold absolute sway over the town, turning it into one of hell's most dedicated outposts on earth.

Sindie's sadness over Micah was swept away as the mass proceeded to the stage of revelry and orgy. She indulged in the delights of the flesh with her usual wild abandon, losing herself in the sheer sensory overload of it all as the midnight air thickened with black, swirling smoke and the stench of burning human flesh.

EPILOGUE

Three months later

Scarlet Collins was back in Littleburg after a semester away at the community college in Monroe County. She had mixed feelings about being back in her hometown. The place was as quiet as ever, but something felt different. A lot of people she'd known growing up here were no longer around, including a few who'd been close friends. She was given conflicting reasons for the mini-exodus every time she inquired about it. For her that was clue enough to *stop* inquiring about it. She knew the town had a dark underbelly. There'd been whispered rumors about sinister happenings in the woods on the outskirts of town for as long as she could remember. She didn't know how much stock she put in the rumors, but it'd long been understood it was best not to get too nosy about it.

In the end, she decided to accept the multiple disappearances as just part of life in Littleburg. There wasn't a lot going on around here in terms of fun things to do. It was a boring place, really. That some of the town's denizens would opt to suddenly leave and start over somewhere else was no big surprise.

Scarlet was just glad she'd been able to rent her old apartment from the Dozier family again. The room above their garage was more or less as she'd left it at the end of the previous summer. The walls were still adorned with her collection of horror movie posters. Right now, as she sat atop chubby Franklin Beauchamp on her bed and rode his big dick in a slow, rhythmic way, she had a direct view of the posters for *The Texas Chainsaw Massacre* and *The Evil Dead*. Both movies were perennially in her top five horror films of all-time. Top five films *period*, actually. These posters occupied wall space above her wall-mounted 55-inch television, which was currently tuned to Channel 39.

She began to ride Franklin faster when she heard the familiar *Shock Theater* theme music emanate from the soundbar. The show had been one of her favorites since childhood. It had been on hiatus for a while, however, because the old Count Gravemore guy was one of the many who'd disappeared in her absence. The show had been gone entirely during that time. Not a single rerun had aired, from what she'd been told.

Now, apparently, it was back.

But, as she soon learned, this was no rerun.

The distinctive organ-driven theme music ended and the cheesy old-school title graphics gave way to a shot of a completely redesigned set for the show. The old set's vibe had been very Hammer Films, but this new one looked like it was inspired by the likes of *Hostel* and *Saw*. It had a grimy industrial look and featured graphically realistic depictions of bodies locked into various torture devices. A woman in a tiny black dress stood between two of these devices. Her back was turned to the camera. Then she turned around and smiled as she appeared to lick blood from the blade of a butcher knife. The blood was probably the usual stage mixture of red food coloring and Karo syrup, but it looked good on screen.

Bouncing up and down on Franklin with even greater vigor now, Scarlet gasped and pointed at the screen. "Holy shit! I know that chick! She works at that record store on Main Street. Or she used to anyway."

Franklin said something, but it was muffled by the studded black bondage mask encircling his head.

On the screen, the camera zoomed in for a closer shot of the new host of *Shock Theater*. "Good evening," she purred in the silkiest, sexiest voice Scarlet had ever heard. "And welcome to *Shock Theater*. I'm Sindie Midnight, your new host. Tonight we bring you a blood-curdling double feature of glorious Satanic majesty, beginning with *Blood On Satan's Claw*."

"*Yes!*"

Scarlet's exclamation was partially a product of sexual excitement, but it was also fueled by the pure joy she felt over the return of *Shock Theater*. She rode Franklin harder and harder, eliciting more muffled complaints from beneath the bondage mask. Franklin sounded like he was in a lot of pain, which was to be expected with so many strands of barbed wire holding his limbs in place. It was amazing how impressively hard a tortured man could stay after being force-fed so many boner pills. She'd been riding him for almost an hour and his dick was still just as engorged as it had been at the beginning.

She figured she'd keep at it at least until the resuscitated *Shock Theater* went to its first commercial break. Then she might start working on him with the knife. It was a funny thing. During her time away from Littleburg, her murderous compulsions had gone away, but the old craving for blood came back within days of her return. There was just something about this place.

Something that made her feel … *evil.*

ACKNOWLEDGMENTS

I'd like to thank C.V. Hunt and Andersen Prunty for their hard work in getting this book out in a greatly accelerated time frame. They kick a frankly astonishing amount of ass. Brian Keene, Ryan Harding, Matt Hayward, Mike Lombardo, Tod Clark, and my brother Jeff are some other cool people I know. Of course, I have to thank my wife, Jenn, because she's fucking awesome. Last but definitely not least, huge thanks go out to my Patreon "super supporters": Brian Keene, Brian W. Picard Sr., Ben Ohmart, Jordan Lindsey, Joe Brannon, Robert Witherington, Scott Berke, and Tim Feely.

Look at that. Brian Keene got named twice in the space of one acknowledgments page. That may be some kind of historical first.

ABOUT THE AUTHOR

Bryan Smith is the author of numerous novels and novellas, including *68 Kill*, *Slowly We Rot*, *Depraved*, *The Killing Kind*, *The Freakshow*, and *Last Day*. Bestselling horror author Brian Keene described *Slowly We Rot* as, "The best zombie novel I've ever read." A film version of 68 KILL, directed by Trent Haaga and starring Matthew Gray Gubler from CRIMINAL MINDS, was released in 2017. Bryan lives in Tennessee with his wife, Jennifer, and their many pets.

Follow him on Twitter at @Bryan_D_Smith and on Facebook at
www.facebook.com/bryansmith/

Get access to exclusive Bryan Smith fiction at Patreon. Includes serialized novellas and novels, excerpts, short stories, and behind-the-scenes essays:

www.patreon.com/horrorauthorbryansmith

Other Grindhouse Press Titles